Call Fitz

By
Debra Gaskill

To Lesa —
Enjoy!
D. Gaskill

ISBN: 978-1512114027

Published by D'Llama Publishing, Enon, Ohio
Cover photo courtesy of Shutterstock

Chapter 1

Gina Cantolini was a whore, but she didn't deserve to die like that. I mean, the girl had a lot of friends.

It was Fawcettville's annual Italian Fest, where they closed down four city blocks and the scent of marinara, cannoli and cheap Chianti hung like a fog around the stone Civil War soldier standing at attention in the center of the square. Every wop or wannabe in town was there.

Which was amazing because nobody ever saw Gina's bloody body underneath the bandstand set up in the middle of the street. Her sandal-clad foot must have stuck out from beneath the canvas skirt at the back of the stage for hours.

It doesn't say much for me, the only PI in town, that I didn't see it either, even as I leaned out the office window to look out over the crowd, a bottle of Jack and a glass sitting on the sill.

My office is up above Grundy's Fine Watches and Jewelers on the town square. It's not much to look at, all dark wood, used furniture and bad paint straight out of a film noir. Since my wife dumped me, I've been sleeping on the waiting room couch at night, eating at a variety of downtown diners and showering at the YMCA after my morning workout.

That night, blue, flashing lights woke me up about 1 a.m. I looked out the window to see a couple of cruisers and the coroner's van behind what was left of the bandstand. I wasn't on that payroll anymore, so I didn't give a shit. I'd made it through the requisite twenty years it took to get a cop's pension. I went back to sleep.

Police picked up the suspect, Michael Atwater, within a few hours after finding the body, according to the TV news the next morning. I knew Atwater from my days on the force. A really stupid kid whose decent, hardworking parents didn't raise him to do all this dumb shit, Atwater wasn't the type to kill anybody, but you never know. Maybe he tried to steal Gina's purse and she fought back. Maybe he wanted something that wasn't on Gina's usual menu, or maybe he just refused to pay and things got out of hand. Either way, a twenty-five-year-old hooker was dead and a small-time thug was behind bars for her murder.

Seemed pretty cut and dried.

And, again, not my problem.

So, two days later, I was surprised when his attorney, James Ambrosi, Esquire, was waiting in the hall at my office door when I got back from the Y. He was leaning against the wall, reading email on his smartphone.

"So, Jimbo," I said, pulling the office key from my hoodie pocket and sliding it into the lock. "What brings you here?"

Ambrosi was closer to the end of his mediocre legal career than the beginning. He was a slob, like his clients, and his breath smelled like convenience store cigars. His suits were cheap, what was left of his comb-over was gray and he stood too close to you during conversations. He was on the lower rungs on the town's legal ladder, the kind of lawyer who could get a halfway decent plea agreement negotiated for you, but probably couldn't be counted on to provide a stellar defense.

In all my years on the force, I spent a lot of time in courtrooms, explaining how or why the asshole at the defense table ended up there. I don't think Ambrosi cross-examined me more than a handful of times and every time his client ended up doing hard time.

Me, I didn't do a lot of defense work in my newest profession.

Most of my clients were suburban wives with enough money to pay me to verify what they knew in their hearts: hubby had a little something on the side. If it wasn't the wives themselves that called me, it was their lawyers. Most of the wives wanted to pay me back the same way their husbands had betrayed them.

It's why I'm sleeping on the waiting room couch.

Ambrosi didn't speak as we walked through the door. I tossed my gym bag into the corner, next to an end table filled with old *Field and Stream* magazines.

"Coffee?" I asked. As he followed me into the office, I shoved a cup his direction, so as to keep his cigar breath at arm's length.

"Sure." Ambrosi accepted my offering and sank into one of the ratty chairs in front of my desk.

I poured myself a cup and sat down, feeling like I'd dodged a halitosis bullet.

"So, what brings you here?" I repeated.

"Mike Atwater, the kid they picked up for Gina Cantolini's murder."

"You representing him?" *Poor kid. You'd think his parents would find a real lawyer.*

"Uh huh." Ambrosi took a sip of his coffee. "You know me, Fitz, I don't give a shit one way or the other if my client is guilty or innocent. I just want him to get a decent defense."

"Of course. I understand." I nodded. With the least amount of effort on your part, I'm sure.

"And we both know that most of the clients that troop through my office probably did it. This time, though, I think this guy's innocent. I need somebody to look into what's going on. Naturally, your esteemed firm of Fitzhugh Investigations came to mind immediately."

"You know most of my stuff is matrimonial, right?"

"You could do this, Fitz. I know you could, you being a retired cop and all."

I flipped the daily pages on my desktop calendar. Cases were a little thin right now—the blank pages confirmed that. I could use the money, especially if I needed to pay for my own divorce lawyer.

"Why do you think this kid is innocent?" I asked.

Ambrosi sank into the shoulders of his cheap suit and sighed.

"He wouldn't kill Gina. He's the father of two of her three children."

"He is? I did not know that. But, sad to say, it happens all the time." I shrugged.

"But my client was crazy about Gina and crazy about those two kids."

I shrugged again. "Doesn't mean they couldn't have argued and it got violent. Were they living together?"

"No. She's no Sunday school teacher—we both know that. She had another boyfriend. Maybe a third, both of them violent."

"Give me their names." I pulled a pencil out of my desk drawer and found a piece of scrap paper on the desk.

"Poole. Jacob Poole—that's the one my client told me about. She had a restraining order against him and he's the father of one of her kids."

"So who's the other one?"

"My client claims it's a cop."

I arched an eyebrow. Chief Nathaniel Monroe hated my guts—and I hated his.

The reason I'm sleeping on the waiting room couch was the same reason my career at the police force ended. Women and an inability to say no to them at one time were the reason I got discharged from the air force (the wing commander's wife) and, in college, why I lost my scholarship (the football coach's wife).

I left the Fawcettville police force after getting caught with the luscious and lonely Mrs. Maris Monroe.

The chief was going to fire me, but I filed my retirement papers twenty minutes before he called me into his office. He'd been gunning for me ever since. It wasn't my fault he couldn't keep his wife happy in the sack. I wasn't the first—I was just the first to get caught.

What if Monroe had a crooked cop on his staff that killed a hooker? I'd love to embarrass that bastard one more time.

"I'll take the case."

*****

The next day, I walked the three blocks from my office to meet Ambrosi and my newest client at the county jail.

Fawcettville was one of those eastern Ohio towns that had weathered more than one economic rise and fall, and it showed. The first economic wave brought the Irish, along with Eastern European and Italian immigrants, like my ancestors, to work in the potteries, making the dishes that filled kitchens all over the world, making Fawcettville famous—and prosperous. When the potteries shuttered their doors, the wops and the polacks, the krauts and the micks all found work in the blast furnaces and the foundries of the steel mills that sprang up in the triangle between Akron, Pittsburgh and Steubenville.

When I was a kid, most people worked in the steel mills. My dad, Sgt. Aidan Fitzhugh was a beat cop, like his dad and his dad before that. We were the only Irish family in the Italian neighborhood everyone called New Tivoli and my Ma, Maria Gallione Fitzhugh made Sunday dinners of pasta, drowning in marinara and meatballs, washed down with gallons of dago red wine.

It was Ma who insisted I carry her father Niccolo's name. In a tough Italian neighborhood in a tougher Ohio steel town, a kid named Niccolo Fitzhugh got made fun of a lot—"Nick the Mick" was the most common taunt my small, scrawny self endured. Then puberty discovered me and I discovered high school football and the weight room. "Nick the Mick" became Fitz.

Neighborhoods back then were marked by their ethnicities. The krauts, the Poles and the hunkies lived in the Flats, down by the creek that ran through town. The hillbillies, the blacks and the Mexicans lived out toward the edge of town in a ratty neighborhood that edged next to the mills and the industrial area, called Tubman Gardens.

Farther away from the creek, up the steep eastern Ohio hills that rose above Fawcettville, was where the mills' executives and middle management lived. The doctors, the lawyers, folks with degrees and letters after their names, lived up those hills in big sprawling houses. It was a symbol that you made it when you could leave the old bricked streets, with their wooden houses and tiny yards and move to the suburbs on the hills.

Then that light, too, went out when I was in high school. The mills closed and Fawcettville got real ugly real fast. Most everyone began referring to it as “F-Town,” for obvious reasons. It was fucked economically.

Back then, the downtown was filled with the dirty windows of the empty storefronts that housed abandoned cobweb-laced display cabinets and peeling paint. I was running from that all those years ago when, after losing my Kent State football scholarship, I got on a bus for Lackland Air Force Base and a hitch in the air force. When I came back in the eighties, things were looking up yet again. This time I had my training as a security policeman in my back pocket and, thanks to Dad, a job on the Fawcettville police department waiting on me.

I looked up at what used to be Kleinman's, Department Store as I strolled toward the jail. Thanks to the latest economic incarnation, the search for natural gas deep in the shale beneath the ground, money was flowing back into Fawcettville. Kleinman's was now broken down into a series of artist's studios, where every wannabe Da Vinci and Grandma Moses could set up their easel and paint for a small rental fee. Their art filled the windows of the first floor gallery, some of it exceptional, most of it crap.

I turned the corner and passed the Mexican joint named for Lupe, the owner's daughter; she automatically opens a cold Dos Equis for me when I walk in the door. Next to the Mexican diner sat a drug store, a tattoo parlor and a cellphone store. There was Horvath's, a coffee shop known for its Hungarian pastries and across the street sat the old jail, built shortly before the Civil War soldier was ensconced in the center of town.

I stopped in front of the old Victorian structure, which was now a four-star restaurant called Ye Olde Gaol. I jammed my hands in my pants pocket and sighed.

Six years ago, I'd asked Dr. Grace Darcy, Ph.D., to marry me there. She was tough talking, tall, with dark cascading hair and brown eyes that shot with fire when I pissed her off, which was often. As the principal cellist in the Fawcettville symphony and a professor of music at the college, she was infinitely a better catch than I was.

I'd married up, no doubt. How could I have fucked it up so badly?

I shook my head and stepped across the bricked street toward the seventies' era jail, all razor wire and concrete. Michael Atwater and his illustrious legal representative were waiting for me there.

Chapter 2

Atwater looked scared, scared as any dumbass should have been. I saw it in his eyes as Ambrosi and I walked into the conference room where he sat waiting on us.

His leg was shackled to the ring in the floor and his hands were cuffed as a deputy stared at him from his chair in the opposite corner. The sheriff's office would have claimed that was "customary procedure," but the truth was Fawcettville didn't get a whole lot of homicides over the course of a year and they wanted to look good.

Atwater's orange prison garb nearly matched his ginger hair and the two-days' growth of beard on his face. His looks were fading from back in the day when I'd arrested him more than a time or two, starting back when he was in juvie. If his parents had a bigger influence than the scum buckets he'd chosen to run around with, Michael Atwater might have been a family man by now, working in somebody's machine shop, paying his bills. Guess that's what happens when you work harder at being a fuck-up than getting a job.

"Fitz." The deputy nodded at me as he walked toward the door.

"Gardosi," I replied.

"So how's business? Maris Monroe still paying you well?" He smirked.

Amazing how small towns never forget—or forgive—a sin. Maris Monroe was seven years ago, a full year before I married Grace.

"No, Gardosi," I said, setting my briefcase on the conference table and staring him dead in the eye. "I've moved on. To your wife."

Gardosi slammed the door as Atwater smirked, relieved not to be the object of attention for a moment.

Jim Ambrosi sighed heavily as he sat down across from his client.

"Michael, this is Mr. Fitzhugh," Ambrosi began. Even across the table, I could smell his cheap cigars.

Atwater tried to stand to shake my hand, but his manacles wouldn't let him. I waved him back down into his seat.

"We've met," I said. "Trust me. So tell me, Mikey, why you shouldn't be convicted of killing Gina Cantolini."

Ambrosi shoved the original police report my way and I took a few minutes to read it.

According to the report, the victim's body was found when organizers began to tear down the bandstand a little after midnight. She had been strangled and beaten, but not near the bandstand. Her cheap Wal-Mart top was torn, either as she was trying to escape or as she was initially grabbed. There were no fingerprints, so investigators surmised her attacker wore gloves or wiped the body clean before leaving it beneath the stage. She was also shot once in the chest with a .38.

Time of death was estimated to be about ten p.m. Investigators were still looking to find out where exactly Gina Cantolini was murdered. They were also still looking for the gun.

Her purse was found dumped in the alley behind the Mexican restaurant, the cash gone.

One of the festival organizing committee remembered seeing her earlier in the evening with a redheaded guy who fit Atwater's description. They had been arguing.

When the suspect was found at home in his second-floor apartment six blocks away, he was passed out on the couch with scratch marks on both arms and a bloody lip. Two hundred dollars was wadded up in the pocket of his jeans and a still-glowing joint was burning into the edge of the coffee table. The only lawful thing Atwater did was now biting him in the ass: his legally registered .38 was missing.

I shoved the report back at Ambrosi.

"Doesn't look good," I said.

"But I didn't do it!" Atwater cried.

"You were seen arguing with the victim." I began to tick off on my fingers all the reasons why any jury would convict him.

"She told me my boys weren't mine! I got served with a warrant for my DNA!" Atwater cried. "I was pissed off!"

"A lot of men would kill if they learned their children weren't theirs," I said, ticking off another finger. "You're also behind on child support payments. I could understand that. Why make payments on kids that aren't yours?"

"I tried to give her money Saturday. She wouldn't take it."

"Two hundred dollars?" I asked. "How do we know that money wasn't in her wallet to begin with? What man would allow the woman he loves to work as a hooker?"

"No, no, no. That's not true." Atwater shook his head in denial. "The money was mine, and I wanted to give it to her."

"You are aware child support payments need to be made through the courts," I said. "That protects you as well as her. How far behind are you?"

Atwater shrugged.

Ambrosi scrawled a number on a piece of paper and shoved it my direction.

"About seven hundred dollars?" I asked, after reading the note.

Again Atwater shrugged.

"And those scratches on your arm, that bloody lip... Did Gina give those to you when she tried to fight you off?"

"Naw, I fell."

I arched an eyebrow.

"No, seriously, I did! I was drunk and high down at the festival and I tripped over a curb."

"You were seen arguing with the victim, who told you recently the children you believed were yours might belong to another man. You've got cuts and scratches all over you and I'm supposed to believe you tripped on a curb? To add to it, the gun she was shot with is the same caliber as one registered to you and is now conveniently missing. If I were a juror, it looks to me like Gina was fighting back. You're behind on your child support payments and you have a long criminal history, for everything from drugs, to burglary to assault and domestic violence and that's just what I can remember. When did I first arrest you, Mikey? When you were eleven? I'll bet the jury wouldn't be out more than twenty minutes."

"Mr. Fitzhugh—Fitz—"Atwater stammered as he reached for my arm. "I didn't kill Gina. I wouldn't have done that. We all know Gina weren't perfect, but I loved her. I loved her like I ain't never loved nobody else. And I loved them two boys, too! They was my whole life! Look at Jacob Poole and look at that cop! They're the ones what killed her!"

"What cop are you talking about?" I asked. Monroe had a lot of good guys on the force, but there were always a couple assholes, no matter where you worked.

"Whaddaya mean, *what* cop?" Atwater's shackles chimed as he threw up his hands.

"There's thirty-six full-time patrol cops in Fawcettville, four detectives, the chief, the assistant chief, Lieutenant Baker, two sergeants and nine dispatchers. That's fifty-four folks," I said. "I think you understand I need you to be a little more specific."

Atwater leaned toward me. "The big guy. The black guy."

"Brewster? *Mac* Brewster?" I was incredulous. The guy had been a patrol officer for years. He was known in the community for his work with the kids in the Tubman

Gardens neighborhoods, active in his church, and an all-around good guy. He even coached a Special Olympics softball team, for Christ sake.

Atwater nodded at me somberly, but didn't say a word.

"What did Brewster do to Gina?"

"She told me there was a cop who would come over to her house and ask for, um, stuff."

"What kind of stuff?"

"You know. *Sex stuff.* If she wouldn't do it, he would threaten to arrest her."

I looked at Ambrosi, who nodded. For once, I could see why Ambrosi wanted me on the case. This stinking sloppy has-been really *did* believe his client was innocent.

"What about Jacob Poole?" I asked. "What's his connection to Gina?"

"He is the father of the victim's other child, the daughter," Ambrosi said slowly. "There is a history of domestic violence there as well. She currently has a restraining order against him, but it gets broken on a regular basis."

"He breaks it or she does?"

"They both do," Ambrosi said.

I understood. This whole domestic violence thing usually put the cops in a bad position when a call from a hysterical female came in. I'd seen enough situations to know that the blame could sometimes be spread around equally. I'm not saying women deserved to get beat—not at all. People need to know how to work things out by talking, sure. I'm just saying that it was rarely the clear-cut situation when Johnny thought Maria deserved a black eye because his spaghetti wasn't *al dente* again. It was just easier when I was on the force to arrest them both and let the lawyers fight it out.

"OK. Let me do some investigation and I'll let you know," I made a few notes and shoved them into my briefcase.

I stood up and Atwater grabbed my hand.

"You gotta find out the truth, Mr. Fitzhugh. I didn't kill Gina. I didn't kill her."

Something in the stupid kid's eyes made me want believe him, despite all the damning evidence. I only hoped Ambrosi's check didn't bounce when this stupid kid's hope gave way to disappointment. It wasn't my job to believe in somebody. It was my job to find out the truth.

*****

Back at the office, I fired up my laptop and searched the clerk of courts web site for arrest records on two of the parties involved in Gina's death.

Gina's legal source of income was her monthly welfare check and had been for years. Her vice was liquor and pills. When there was more month left at the end of her money, she turned to hooking. More than once I'd seen her working some of the downtown bars.

No doubt she'd started life like every child did, all smiles and hope for the future. Then somewhere along the line, something happened. She discovered booze and barbiturates, enough to numb whatever was eating her from inside, and nobody ever knew what. Of course, nobody In Fawcettville ever cared to ask. As long as Gina didn't bring her addictions and her illegitimate babies to their neighborhood, but left it all on the outer edges of the Flats, the house-proud Italians of New Tivoli didn't want to know about Gina Cantolini.

Gina's arrest record bounced between prostitution, public indecency, public intoxication, and domestic violence, peppered with a couple misdemeanor-shoplifting charges. In several of the public intox and the domestic violence incidents, Jacob Poole and Michael Atwater were also arrested.

Between the three of them, I could see a dysfunctional love triangle of drinking, fighting and making up. What was her hold over those two men? Her kids? Her bed?

The office door clicked open and I looked up from my computer.

Dammit.

"Hey, baby," Maris Monroe slid one round hip over the corner of my desk and leaned over to move one of my graying black curls from my forehead. She smiled and made sure I got a good look at what filled her low-cut top.

I leaned back in my chair.

"What are you doing here?" I asked.

"I heard you were at the jail today." She hoisted the rest of her behind onto my desk and swung her long, tanned legs toward me, moving smoothly and quickly enough for me to get a quick shot of red panties beneath her too-short black skirt. Her curly brown hair was tied back in a ponytail.

Maris was the Chief's second wife, arm candy fifteen years his junior he thought he needed to share his golden years with, not the woman who raised his children and helped him move up the career ladder. Now he was saddled with a barracuda he couldn't control and couldn't afford to dump.

"So? Who told you?"

She reached over again, and tousled my graying hair. "A little bird."

"You don't need to be here, Maris." I patted my mop back into place.

"Oh, come on, Fitz. You know you're the only one I want." She pushed the laptop back so she could scoot directly in front of me, giving me another shot of those red panties.

"Go home, Maris."

"I heard you were staying here now, all by yourself." Maris leaned close, close enough for me to smell her perfume. Her words were a soft and sultry whisper. I shut my eyes and clenched my fists. In another life, I'd already have my hands up that skirt and we'd be halfway to paradise.

Not now. Not ever again.

"You need to be home with your husband. Grace and I are still trying to work things out."

Maris sat back and crossed her legs, smirking.

"Really? I hear she might have another opinion of that."

"What do you mean?"

"I hear she's stepping out. I hear Dr. Grace has a date this weekend."

"With who?"

Sit back, old man. She could be baiting you. It could be a lie.

Maris shrugged. "Somebody with the college, maybe. Somebody with the symphony—I don't know. I just heard she had an escort to this weekend's benefit."

The annual symphony benefit was one of Fawcettville's social highlights, when the community's leading lights came down from their hillside homes, the last event before Fawcettville's long hot summer. The chief would be there, along with the mayor and city council, and the town's big donors. I'd forgotten it was this weekend. Grace got me into a tuxedo five years running for the event. She'd always looked striking in whatever gown she'd chosen.

I closed my eyes and remembered those nights after the benefit was over and the gown was in a wad on the floor.

"Grace wouldn't do that to me."

"Oh she wouldn't, huh? You're sure about that?" Maris slipped off the desk, tucked her black leather designer bag beneath her arm and walked toward the door. "When you figure out that she's moved on, I'll be waiting," she called back over her shoulder.

And she was gone.

I pulled the laptop back from the edge of the desk and sighed. Grace wouldn't be going to the benefit without me, would she? She couldn't be dating already, right?
I tried to focus on Jacob Poole's court record, but couldn't do it. After a couple hours, I hit the power button on the laptop and shut the lid.

Go ask her. Head over to the college and find out. If she were dating somebody, she'd tell you.

If she is, that means it's really over, my heart answered.

I had to know. Maris Monroe would lie to me, just to get me back in the sack and twist my life up more than it already was. I didn't need that kind of poison in my life. Rather than believe Maris, I'll go straight to the source. Good thing about the Internet, it was open all night. I could finish my research on Atwater, Poole and Cantolini later. I needed to talk to Grace *now*.

I slid on my hoodie and walked out the door. I turned to lock the door when a thick hand grabbed my collar, shoving my face against the doorframe. I felt the cold barrel of a gun between my shoulder blades. Any sudden move I made toward my Glock .45 caliber, tucked into the shoulder holster inside my hoodie, would not have ended well. I let my hands hug the wall.

"I wouldn't move, if I were you." The voice was deep and raspy, one I couldn't recognize.

"I never touched her—I don't care what she told you," I answered.

"Huh?" The hand at the base of my skull released for a minute and I tried to turn to get a look at my attacker. The goon pushed back, slamming my face into the door again, making me see stars.

"Maris Monroe. She was here earlier. I told her to go home to her husband," I said, tasting blood inside my mouth. "I never touched her."

"I don't give a rat's ass about your women. It's that case you took." The gun barrel pushed harder in between my shoulders.

"What about it?"

"Drop it. Drop it now."

"Why? What's it to you?"

"I'm just here to deliver a message."

The gun butt came down hard on the back of my head and as I fell to the floor, the lights went out.

Chapter 3

The hallway was bathed in the sun's last orange gasps when I came to and pushed myself up off the dirty floor. I touched the goose egg on the back of my head as I stood. *Shit, that hurts.* It wasn't bleeding, unlike the inside of my mouth. I ran my tongue along my teeth—at least they were all there.

I patted myself down, searching—thank God, the Glock was still inside my hoodie. I pulled it out of my shoulder holster and checked the clip. No bullets were missing; everything looked good. I shoved it back inside my jacket.

Why would someone want me off the Cantolini case? A hooker is dead and her loser boyfriend is in jail. This certainly doesn't involve anybody who mattered in Fawcettville. So who was sending a message? And why?

The mob? Nah. After too much *vino*, everybody in New Tivoli bragged they had out-of-town family who were mobbed up, but nobody believed it. Organized crime was for towns like Cleveland, Pittsburgh and Youngstown, not small towns like Fawcettville. This was where the working-class stiffs came to get their tiny piece of the fading American dream. Besides, Gina Cantolini's family didn't even live here anymore. If they had and if they were mobbed up, two things would have happened: she would have been married off quickly or her baby daddy's body would have been found in the trunk of his own car and she would have been set up as a cute young widow somewhere out of state.

I continued to think as I walked down the stairs to the square, where my black Excursion was parked. I slid into the driver's seat, catching a glimpse of a bruised and scratched left cheek and a blackening eye in the rearview. *Great. That must have happened when I got slammed against the doorframe.*

I didn't have many dealings with Poole during my days on the force, maybe an occasional bar fight or public intoxication. Other cops, though, told me he could be a real bastard and I knew through them he could be violent.

Could the man who cold-cocked me have been Poole? Why would it be him? The other man in his woman's life is on ice and most likely would be convicted. If Poole were smart, he'd sit back and keep his mouth shut. There was no need to smack an investigator in the skull.

And Mac Brewster? *C'mon.* I wasn't even going to waste my time on that Boy Scout. No way Mac could be dirty. His intention of getting Gina Cantolini in a room alone would probably be to get her to turn her life over to Jesus. Whatever Gina was telling Michael Atwater about Mac was more than likely a lie.

I needed to think a little bit more about which way to go on this case.

But first, I needed to see Grace. I slipped my key into the car ignition and pulled into traffic.

*****

The symphony was rehearsing down at Memorial Hall, where this weekend's benefit would be held. Grace was sitting in the center of the stage alone, playing the prelude to Bach's *Cello Suite No. 1*. The other symphony musicians milled around the jumble of the chairs and music stands on the stage or sat listening in the first few rows of seats.

A single spotlight reflected blue highlights off her dark curly hair and regal cheekbones. Her eyes were closed in concentration as her body swayed with each draw of her bow. She wore a white camisole beneath a gauzy white shirt that didn't restrict her movements; tight jeans accentuated her long legs.

In her presence, I always felt troll-like. Maybe I was: no neck, big shoulders, thick bowed legs and standing at the higher end of short, I had my father's round pugilist's face, my mother's dark Italian hair and her father's big chest. My nose reflected my football and personal career: it was slightly off center from more than one break. For some reason, women liked me. I wasn't a slob like Ambrosi though, I kept my gut in check during my daily workouts, and got my back waxed regularly at Gracie's insistence. If she asked, I'd dye my graying hair for her.

I still wore a stained Kent State Football hoodie, despite being kicked off the team some thirty-plus years ago, clinging to it, Gracie said, like a toddler's security blanket.

I sat down toward the back in one of the aisle seats and watched, transfixed, as she coached the mellow tones from her cello. The other musicians were drawn in, too, with each note. Before long the idle conversation stopped as the music swelled and rolled through the hall. With a final flourish of Grace's bow, a last, rich note hung in the air for a moment and faded.

Automatically, I stood and walked from the back of the hall, clapping. Others on stage also applauded, joining the musicians in the seats. I was halfway down the aisle, ready to call out her name as the applause died down.

But the ovation didn't come to a complete stop. One tall thin man, wearing black pants and a gray shirt, walked from the back of the stage, clapping slowly. His brown hair was just starting to gray and his hands looked soft. He had a sweater across his shoulders and his expensive shoes shone. Grace turned around as he approached and smiled at him.

Who is this asshole? My stomach dropped. Maybe Maris Monroe was right.

He leaned over the music stand and ran his finger across the top of the sheet music. It didn't take much for me to imagine him running that same finger down her naked spine in the bed we once shared.

"Good job, Dr. Darcy," he said.

She tipped her chin up toward him and beamed. *OK, this shit's got to stop.* I stepped into the light. A few other musicians recognized me. They stepped back out of my way, their eyes widening. Apparently our marital discord was no secret.

"Yes, my *wife* is an excellent musician," I said loudly.

Grace stood and waved Rico Suave away. "Give me a minute," she said softly.

Quickly, he and the other musicians disappeared from the hall. Grace lay her cello down on its side and walked to the edge of the stage, holding the bow. She sat down, letting her feet in their gold ballet flats hang over the ledge. I walked nearer, opening my arms. She jabbed the bow into the center of my chest like a rapier. No surprise there—Grace was also the college's women's fencing coach.

I stopped in my tracks. She laid the bow beside her on the stage, but I didn't dare come closer.

"You're still doing time for me, aren't you, Nicco?" She was the only one who called me by my first name. I'd never been just Fitz to Grace.

"Who's he?" I jerked my thumb toward Rico Suave, who stood just offstage, his arms crossed. His icy blue eyes were trained on me.

"He's Peter Van Hoven, the new conductor," she said. "This weekend's benefit is also a welcome for him."

"Looks like you've already made him feel quite at home." Like some baton-waving Nancy boy could scare me. *Meet me in the alley motherfucker,* I wanted to say, *I'll kick your ass.*

"What do you expect me to do? Sit around like a nun until you figure out how to sign the divorce papers?" She raised one hand to write in the air.

"Gracie, please." I stepped closer and got the bow in the chest again. "Ouch!"

"No. I was warned when I started dating you and I didn't listen. 'He's as faithful as a tomcat,' she said. 'Don't let him break your heart.' "

"Who said that?"

"Your *mother.*"

I sighed. "She's been pissed off since I told her I wasn't going to be a priest and wanted to play football." My three brothers, Aidan, Jr., Randy, and Mateo and two sisters, Christina and Mary Katherine, all had large Irish-Italian Catholic families. The fact that I didn't get married until my early fifties kept her hope alive that someone from the family would don the clerical collar. As always, I disappointed her.

"Nicco, don't jerk me around. Just sign the papers and we can both move on with our lives. It's not like we've got any big assets to split."

I moved into Gracie's Tudor home six weeks before our wedding with a single suitcase and the service revolver I got at retirement. When I left, I left with the same things. We had no children's lives to destroy, no dog to argue custody over. Grace was as dedicated to her career as I was to mine, although, if this divorce went through I'd sure as hell miss the cat, Mozart.

"You going out with him?"

"Maybe. That's none of your business. What happened to your face? Did some pissed-off husband find you in one of those dive bars you frequent?"

"No, I fell." She didn't need to know the details. Not now.

"So, are you still seeing her?"

"Gracie, I told you. She was a client. She'd been drinking—she was out of control. I didn't mean for it to happen."

"And I didn't mean to walk into your office at two in the afternoon and find you *in flagrante delicto* at your desk."

My arms sank to my sides. "We weren't—never mind. I know what it looked like." I turned away. "You're right. I can't ask you to live like a nun, just like you said. I'll talk to you later, Gracie. We'll get this worked out."

"Soon?"

"Yeah." I felt like I'd been kicked in the gut. "Soon."

*****

I visited Mike Atwater's parents' house right after my workout the next day. The Atwaters lived outside of Fawcettville in a bungalow that had seen better days. A plaster gnome in a fading red hat and flaking paint sat by the front porch steps, holding a large mushroom with "Welcome" carved into it. On the other side of the step was a deer, equally fading and flaking, with big cartoon eyes and smile. Back in the day, when I'd brought a juvenile Mikey home from whatever late-night scrape I'd found him in, the bungalow was better kept than the others in the working-class cluster of homes up and down the road. Today, the yard hadn't been mowed in a long, long time and weeds grew through holes in rusting metal barrels along the driveway. The paint was chipped and there was cardboard in one of the upstairs windows.

A tall, rawboned woman opened the door. Her graying hair was trying to escape from the haphazard bun on top her head; her jeans were faded and the sleeves on her Steelers sweatshirt were pushed up her scrawny arms.

She had the look of a woman who was used to bill collectors coming to her door—or the police coming to see her about her kid.

"If you're a reporter, I'm done talking to reporters," she said flatly.

"Susan Atwater?" I handed her a business card. "I'm Nick Fitzhugh, Fitzhugh Investigations. Mike's attorney sent me. I was wondering if you had some time to talk to me?"

"Jim Ambrosi?" Susan leaned out the door and looked from left to right. I nodded. She waved me inside. We walked wordlessly through the scruffy living room toward the kitchen; Susan pointed to a wooden chair that didn't match the others surrounding the worn, scratched table. She took a seat across from me and pulled a green melamine ashtray toward her. Smoke from a lone cigarette wafted in lazy spirals toward the ceiling. Susan looked at it sadly before picking it up and inhaling.

"I suppose you want to know what kind of an awful mother I was to have a kid who ends up in jail for murder," she said, raising her chin and exhaling.

"No ma'am," I said, pulling a notebook from my hoodie pocket. "I want to know about Gina and Michael's relationship."

Years ago, Susan Atwater hadn't looked so ragged. Unfortunately, she and her husband Bill always managed to catch a ride in the last car of the latest economic roller coaster, the last of the working poor who saw benefit from any rising financial tide. From Ambrosi, I learned Bill lost his job in the 2008 crash. Susan had worked as a cashier at the grocery store for years but they had no savings and no retirement accounts, having spent them bailing out their son on more than one occasion.

Bill's new job in the Pennsylvania shale fields started recently and he only made it home on the weekends. Susan was still working at the grocery store to keep herself busy while Bill was gone—and make payments on past due bills.

"That girl." Susan shook her head. "I never liked Gina Cantolini, but you can't ever tell your kids those things. I was the same way. My mama didn't like the boy I came home with—Michael's daddy—and it made me stick to him that much more. We ran off to Jellico, Tennessee and got married when I was fifteen. Michael came along six months later. Michael's the same way. He fell for that girl and fell bad. I thought I'd be smart when he brought her home, and keep my mouth shut. I saw that girl was nothing but trouble and I never said anything. Maybe I should have."

"What kind of trouble?"

"Mr. Fitzhugh, my boy's no angel. His daddy and me, we did everything we could to keep him on the straight and narrow, but Michael, he went down his own road and none of those roads were the right way. Gina was one bad road all by herself."

I nodded. I wasn't going to tell Susan I knew all about her boy—or his girlfriend. "Why was Gina a bad road?"

Susan took another drag from her cigarette and stubbed it out in the ashtray.

"She'd tell him those two babies were his, then she'd tell him they were Jacob Poole's, then she'd cry and apologize and they'd fight—sometimes she and Michael, sometimes Jacob and Michael. Then somebody—sometimes everybody—would get arrested."

"Whose do you think they are?"

Susan stood and walked to the living room. She came back with two framed photos.

"See this? This was taken about fifteen years ago at a family reunion." She held out a family photo of men of various generations, clustered around an old white-haired man in a recliner, hunched over the oxygen tank in his lap. I picked out Michael, then a surly teen, from among the other older guys, all of them with various shades of the same flaming red hair.

"OK."

"Now look at this one." Susan showed me the other photo. Two children sat on Santa's lap; the photo was snapped as one of the boys howled while the other stared terrified into the camera.

"You see it?" Susan sat the photos down on the kitchen table and picked up her cigarette again, arching her eyebrow. "They both have brown hair, don't they? Ain't no Atwater boy been born without red hair in four generations."

"You don't believe they're your grandchildren, do you?"

She shook her head. "Not by blood, no. But here—" she pounded her chest with her thin, bony hand. "They are."

"Where are the boys?"

"I've got them. They're at school right now. I went to get them the night Gina was killed. Family Services thought it would be best, since they were here a lot of the time anyway."

"Who's got the girl?"

"Jacob does."

"Jacob Poole's family doesn't keep the boys at all?"

"Not since she told them they were Michael's boys. But they were behind the deal to get the DNA testing done."

"Where do they live?"

"Akron, Canton, I don't know exactly. The boys don't know who they are anymore."

"Did you see anything odd when you picked up the boys?"

Susan sighed and was silent for a moment. "I knew what Gina did when money got tight. I wasn't happy about it, so I kept the boys as often as I could, just to make sure they didn't see a lot. But when I went over there to pick those boys up after their mama died, I saw something that really upset me."

"What was that?"

"She'd put locks on the outside of their bedroom doors, so they couldn't get out. Those boys were locked in their bedrooms. She'd put those bolt locks on the outside of their doors, up high where they couldn't reach them. What kind of mother does that? What if that house caught fire?"

"What do you think that meant?" I kept looking at my notebook as I wrote.

"That she was turning tricks inside the house, or selling drugs or something at night and she didn't want those boys to see it. Those locks weren't there last week."

"Do you know anything about a cop who was bothering Gina? Michael claimed she was being harassed by a police officer."

Susan clenched her fists on the tabletop and leaned toward me, her eyes filled with intensity.

"Somebody needs to look into that. One day I was there and this big, black cop just walked into Gina's house, swinging his big ole flashlight and yelling if he didn't get a goddamned blow job right now, he'd be busting somebody for prostitution."

"What happened?" I stopped making notes.

"We were back in the kitchen, but I could see him from where I was sitting. She went running to the front room. I heard her say 'Not now. The boys' grandma is here. Come back later.' And he left. When Gina came back into the kitchen, she was shaking. She said he came by at least once a week asking for sex. Said he'd threaten to beat her up if she didn't give him what he wanted."

"What did he look like?"

"Big wide shoulders. Tall."

"What about his hair?"

"Bald as a cue ball."

Mac Brewster's head didn't have a hair on it.

Chapter 4

"Thank you, Mr. Fitzhugh." The woman behind the glassed window pushed a single ticket through the slot. "And thank you for your support of the Fawcettville symphony."

I was in the grand entrance of Fawcettville's Memorial Hall. I smiled and nodded as I slipped the benefit ticket into my wallet. My tuxedo, rented this year, hung over my arm. Gracie and I may not be going together, but by God, we were going to both be there. I had to see if Van Hoven was really her date for the evening, even if it cost me an arm and a leg. If he were, I would have to accept that it was over between us, and I'd sign those goddamned papers.

In the meantime, I had another appointment. Det. Joe Barnes was one of the few folks left on the force I could still call friend. He knew the truth about Maris Monroe. He was also assigned to Gina's murder. We were supposed to meet at Horvath's, the Hungarian coffee shop.

I was already on my second cup and working my way through a plate of apricot *kiflis* when Barnes slid into the booth seat across from me and signaled the waitress for a cup of coffee.

"Fitz, how's it going? What the hell happened to your face?" Barnes was an old-school detective, the other side of retirement age and he held politically incorrect views that made even a mick like me cringe.

I shrugged. "Nothing that won't heal in a week. You probably heard I'm investigating Atwater's case for the defense."

Barnes barked out a short laugh. "And how's that working for you?"

"He looks guilty as hell to me, too, but I need the money."

"I heard that too."

Why the hell is my personal life the biggest topic in the police department, seven years after I'm gone? I shook my head. I didn't want to feed the department's rumor mill, but Barnes didn't need to know that.

"Anyway," I continued. "I'll go through the motions, look at every angle, just like you probably did and most likely come up with the same conclusions. By the way, Maris Monroe showed up at my office the other day and said she knew I'd been there with Ambrosi, talking to Atwater."

"So?"

"So who is she banging there who would tell her I was there? And why would anybody care?"

Barnes shrugged. "I don't know. I know that the Chief is constantly trying to keep her corralled. There's no respect for Monroe anymore—it's like some game, keeping track of everybody his wife has done. The only thing patrol doesn't do is keep a running list of names on the wall where everybody can see. She's a train wreck and that marriage is a disaster. Talk is, the city manager is thinking about firing him, moving the Assistant Chief into the position."

"Probably a good move. So, what else is going on at the PD? Who all is still around that I worked with?" I didn't look him in the eye as I spun my spoon on the table.

"There's always a few new faces, right out of the academy, but they don't last long. They get training and move on to a bigger department or the sheriff's office—or they become Maris's target and get fired."

"I hope some of the old guard is still around, folks like Mac Brewster?"

"Oh sure. Brewster's still around."

"Still the eternal do-gooder?"

"Yeah. You know Mac—he's trimmed back some of the stuff he's been doing, though. I guess he's still coaching the Special Olympics softball team. He's not the only black face on the force these days."

Jesus, Barnes. I cringed inwardly, but tried to sound nonchalant. "Oh yeah?"

"Yeah, when a new assistant prosecutor came in, she recommended Monroe hire this guy. Former KSU football player, real big guy."

My ears perked up. This could be the cop that Susan and Michael Atwater claimed was demanding sex from Gina.

"Know anything about him?"

Barnes shook his head. "No. I hear he's the boyfriend, and he's a real go-getter. Monroe likes him a lot."

"What's his name?"

"What do you care? You're retired." Barnes arched an eyebrow.

"You're right. I don't care. Just trying to keep up, I guess." Honestly, I was relieved I had someone else to look at other than Mac Brewster. I'd find somebody who knew the name of this new cop. I finished my last *kifli* and my coffee as Barnes rattled on for another twenty minutes about the same shit that he complained about seven years ago: the department secretary who left food in the employee fridge until well past its expiration, the dispatcher who was clear as a bell on the radio but mumbled on the phone, the damage EMTs did to crime scenes.

He stopped yammering when I lay my napkin on the table.

"So, I figured you were going to try and pull information out of me about Atwater." Barnes looked at me over his coffee cup.

I shrugged and leaned back, shoving my hands in my hoodie pockets.

"Isn't that what the discovery process is all about?" I asked. "Don't we play 'I'll show you mine if you show me yours' when the trial date gets closer?"

Barnes smiled. "That's what I always liked about you Fitz. No bullshit, no games."

"Thanks. You guys still trying to find the actual crime scene, right? I read that in the report."

"Yup, and the gun. I think you ought to know though, it still doesn't look good for your boy Atwater. There's too much evidence against him."

"I know."

"There's something else. Have you talked to the prosecutor lately?"

Dennis Lance was a Fawcettville native with bigger aspirations than county prosecutor. Tall, blond and athletic looking, word was that Lance wanted bigger things out of life: a judgeship, maybe state senator eventually. He contributed money to all the right causes and was seen at all the right events, glad-handing everyone in sight.

Lance came to the prosecutor's office right out of law school and stayed, until ten years ago when he decided to run for his boss's job and won. He was a good enough prosecutor, a real bulldog in court, but I never quite trusted his made-for-TV looks and courtroom antics, even though his record of convictions was strong.

I didn't know a whole lot about Lance's personal life, but knew he had a big fancy house with some acreage and a couple horses out in the county. His office was decorated with some of the horse show ribbons he'd won.

"No. Most of my dealings are in family court these days."

"It's been a long, long time since this town's had a homicide," Barnes said. "The common pleas judge is up for reelection this year and from what I hear, Lance is thinking of challenging him for the seat. Lance could be looking at the death penalty on this one, just to make it look like he's tough on crime. This could be the one case Lance hangs his hat on."

"I'll take that under advisement, Detective," I said. "Does Ambrosi know that?"

Barnes shrugged. "I'm assuming so. It would come up in court."

"I'll ask, just for my own information if nothing else."

We laid money on the table to cover our respective orders and walked out the door. Out on the sidewalk, Barnes shook my hand.

"Good luck, Fitz."

"You too, Barnes."

Walking back to my car, I pondered everything Barnes told me. A police department in shambles, thanks to a one-woman wrecking ball, and a prosecutor intent on making a name for himself could spell a lot of trouble for my client, if Michael Atwater was truly innocent. Could either Chief Monroe or Dennis Lance be behind the visitor who decided to christen me outside my office?

That didn't make a lot of sense. Lance didn't need to rely on strong-arm tactics—I'm sure that his arguments for *Ohio v. Atwater* were solid and if he wanted a case to build a political career on, this could be it.

But, if there was anybody who hated me, it was the Chief. As desperate as his situation seemed, maybe the knock on my head really *was* more about Maris's visit and less about the Atwater case—he just wanted it to look like it was. If Monroe was firing young recruits who came into his wife's field of vision, it made sense that he would be going after whomever she was slithering in to see—in this case, me.

I would deal with Maris later. The next thing on the agenda was to find out the name of the new cop on the force and if he was the one who was trying to intimidate Gina Cantolini.

But first, I had to generate some income: a surveillance case, chasing down yet another wayward spouse.

My client suspected her CPA husband of meeting his secretary for quickies on their lunch hour. I'd followed the secretary for two weeks as she went about her life, which didn't show me anything, except that she was extremely health conscious. She was in the Sunrise Yoga class at the YMCA, ran every evening through the park with a yellow Labrador she named Spike and ordered sliced turkey with sprouts, cucumbers and mayo on whole wheat bread at lunch.

The contents of her trashcan showed me someone who followed the stock market through *The Wall Street Journal* and drank cheap bottled water and expensive pinot noir; Spike apparently liked chewing her shoes when bored.

If she was doing her boss, it was happening at the office because it sure wasn't happening at home. I needed to find something one way or another if I wanted to bill the wife's lawyer.

Today, I was going after the CPA. After I left Barnes behind, I dug a pair of binoculars and my camera, with its big zoom lens, out of the back of my Excursion and drove down to the office building, which was out near the mall in a cluster of nondescript office buildings.

The CPA in question drove a bright red Mercedes two-seater, which made it easy to pick out from among the minivans and SUV's in the parking lot.

I pulled the Excursion into the parking lot and slithered down in the seat, binoculars in hand. Before long, my target—a tall brown-haired man with sunglasses—came striding toward the Mercedes. His suit jacket was slung arrogantly across his shoulder and his thumb hooked into the collar; he had the self-confident smile of a man who thought he was getting away with something. He lifted his sunglasses and looked around before sliding into the red car.

I was good at what I did now for a reason—I understood why men chased women… or at least why I'd done it. When I was young, it was all about the chase and the conquest, tapping into the primal hunter that still lurked inside, despite all the socialization we'd been forced into absorbing. As I got older, I realized that it was less the hunt than the connection, finding that one person who'd give life meaning.

I just never knew when to stop looking, until I found Gracie. Or was it when the Chief found me with his wife? I reached over to the passenger seat and pulled the camera over to my lap. I slowly drew the viewfinder up to my eye, focusing on my target.

The CPA sat in the Mercedes, looking left to right, and tapping his fingers on the steering wheel. Suddenly, a tall, blonde woman in a white medical coat came hurriedly into range—it was the orthodontist from the suite next to the CPA's. I knew who she was: as a favor, I'd once taken one of my sister Chrissy's kids to the office for an appointment.

I began to click off shots as she leaned into the driver's side window and planted a big wet one on the number guy's lips, then quickly slid into the passenger side. The CPA fired up the Mercedes and, tires squealing, pulled out of parking lot.

I sat up in my seat, tossing the camera aside and threw the car into drive. I followed the Mercedes at a respectable distance, but close enough to keep an eye on them. The destination wasn't a surprise—one of the motels out by the interstate. They parked in front of the motel room door and slipped out quickly. She already had the room key—maybe she was footing the bill for this assignation since the CPA's wife told me she never found those usual telltale signs of an affair in his finances. The shutter clicked repeatedly as they slipped into the room. An hour later, they came back out: I got shots of her running her hands through his hair as they kissed again. Following them back to the office, I watched as he dropped the orthodontist about a block away before pulling back into the parking lot.

He smirked and smoothed his hair in the rearview mirror. I could tell this was no grand affair to him, no great love he'd stumbled into after years of unhappy marriage.

The lady who straightened pre-teens' teeth for a living was a game to him, a conquest, simply a more interesting way to spend a lunch hour than reading profit and loss statements. When this relationship blew up in his smirking face, he'd move on, dick in hand, to the next woman.

I pulled the blue photo disc out of my camera and put it in an envelope, addressed it to the CPA's wife and headed back to the office.

I called her, told her about my proof and listened to her sob, then dropped the envelope, along with my bill, down the mail slot in the hall.

It seemed a little cold, but I was more than a little leery of having wronged wives in the office these days.

After all, Judith Demyan was the pissed off, half-drunk wife in search of vindication who brought my marriage to its knees less than a month ago.

That day, I had four or five photos spread across my desk, capturing Professor Dave Demyan with his girlfriend, a junior English major at Fawcett University, when Judith burst through the door. She wanted to share a drink with me, to celebrate catching her two-timing husband and her now-impending divorce. She'd already been celebrating when she poured me a couple shots of whiskey from the flask in her purse.

"You know, Fitz, I've always thought you were one sexy bastard." Judith leaned over the desk. I could smell sweet whiskey on her breath.

"Now Judith, Judy—I—I really, I mean, I..." I stuttered like a teenager.

"Oh, silly boy. After what you did for me, I think I owe you a little something special." Judith pushed the photos of her husband and his girlfriend onto the floor. Before I could stop her, she was straddling me in my chair, grinding against my groin as she unbuttoned her blouse.

It didn't look like my hands were meaning to push Judith off my lap when Gracie walked in the door, but that's the truth.

"You dirty son of a bitch!"

I started sleeping on the waiting room couch that very night.

Showing up at the symphony benefit this weekend might seriously piss Gracie off, but it would give me the proof I needed as to whether our marriage had any future or not.

Pensive, I leaned back to look out the window onto the city square.

I sat up sharply—parked just beyond the Civil War soldier was a nondescript four-door sedan with a man wearing all black, leaning on the roof of the car. Long sleeves and a black baseball cap blocked his face as he held binoculars directly aimed at my office.

I threw the window open to get a better look, but the man saw me and jumped into the sedan, speeding off down the street. All I could catch was the first three letters of his Ohio license plate, GRD.

Who the hell was he, and what the hell was going on?

Chapter 5

The sun was setting when I found Mac Brewster at one of the empty Tubman Gardens lots he'd turned into a softball field. He was pitching the ball toward a chunky almond-eyed white boy with thick glasses. The ball connected with the aluminum bat with a low, metallic *tunk* and bounced along the third-base line as the boy ran awkwardly toward first base.

Mac saw me and waved. I stood on the sidelines, behind the parents with their camp chairs and coolers, cheering with them as each child had a chance to hit the ball. From the distance, Mac looked older and more tired. It shouldn't have surprised me; he was on the force when I came on and was still there, pulling the same twelve-hour shifts as everyone else. He never tried for any promotion that I knew of, content to be the best-known, longest serving cop on the beat.

"OK, ya'll, take a break. Get some water." Mac pointed toward the team mother, who smiled broadly as she held up bottled water for the players.

We shook hands and hugged.

"How's it going, Fitz?" he asked.

I shrugged. "It's going. I've been hired to investigate the Atwater case for the defense. Was wondering if you could help me out."

"The kid that killed the hooker? Sad situation." Fitz stuffed his hands in his windbreaker.

"My client says there's been a black cop who was harassing the victim for sex. Big guy. Bald. Says the guy could be the real perp in this mess."

Brewster stepped away. "Don't do this to me Fitz. We go too far back."

"Oh hell, no. I was wondering if you knew anything about anybody new on the force, anybody who's a little shady? I've been gone too long to know everybody these days."

Brewster sighed and shook his head. "It's a mess, Fitz, a sad mess. That department is a shadow of what it used to be."

"Do you know anything about a new recruit who is the boyfriend of the new assistant prosecutor? From what I've heard he fits that description."

"His name is Reno, Reno Elliot. He's rotating through third shift this month."

"Seem OK to you?"

Brewster shrugged again. "I don't know him well enough to say one way or the other. The new recruits come and go so fast these days my head spins."

That was a lie. Mac went out of his way to welcome every new recruit on the force. His wife brought food to cops who had to work holidays, serving them the big homemade meals they were missing.

I shoved my hands deep into the pockets of my hoodie.

"Something about this case stinks, Mac. That's part of the reason I came to you. Maris Monroe shows up at my office after I meet with my client and his attorney, then I get cold-cocked outside my office door. Today, somebody's parked in the square watching my office with binoculars."

Mac was silent for a moment. "Leave it alone, Fitz. Leave it alone."

"Why? What's going on that I should know about?"

"I'm putting my retirement papers in next week. After that, we'll talk." Mac turned back toward his athletes and began clapping his hands. "OK, kids. Let's catch some fly balls!"

He walked away and I shook my head.

Back in my Excursion, I sat and watched Mac work with the kids some more. He had taken the bat himself and

was tossing up the softball and hitting balls—a little harder than necessary I thought—into the outfield for catching practice. He was angry about something.
What happened to the department I'd spent my professional career at?

Nate Monroe was a sergeant when I started at the PD. Dave Stanforth was chief back then. After a few years, Monroe moved up to lieutenant and then assistant chief. When Stanforth dropped dead from a heart attack at fifty-three, Monroe took over as interim and then was appointed by the city manager as the permanent chief.

Somewhere in there, he went crazy with ego. He dumped Darla, his wife of thirty years, and took up with Maris. The divorce was ugly, but everybody has some ugliness somewhere, and cops more than most folks. I don't know if Nate's kids speak to him even today. Needless to say, marrying Maris was a disaster.

But what did that all have to do with Gina Cantolini's murder? That's what I was more concerned about. Was there a dirty cop, as Atwater had implied and as Mac completely avoided? That was just like Mac, though—he wouldn't have said shit about another cop if his mouth were full of it. It made sense that he would talk after he knew his pension was secure. Could I wait that long?

And who was this Reno Elliott? If he was on third shift this month, I knew where I could catch up with him tonight. There was a singular coffee shop called Puccini's that operated all night on the edge of New Tivoli and the downtown. It was a haven for third-shift night owls, especially cops.

Located down the street from my ma's house, I'd worked there as a teenager after school, serving Joe Pucca's famous cannoli, coffee cake, and espresso from behind the red and white Formica counter. I could sit at that same unchanged counter, talking to one of the college students who staffed the place overnight until Reno Elliott came in.

I pulled the Excursion away from the curb and slid into traffic. I had a second appointment—this one with Jacob Poole.

*****

I met Poole at Lupe's, the Mexican restaurant around the corner from the jail. He didn't look up as I slid into the booth seat across from him. He was hunched over his beer, a strand of stringy dirty-blonde hair hanging in his face. He wore his biker leather jacket bearing the Road Anarchy Motorcycle Club logo, scuffed boots, leather gloves without fingers and a perpetually angry expression.

No wonder Susan Atwater didn't want Michael's alleged sons to be carrying this man's DNA: if Poole was their father, neither of those boys had any future. There was slight hope if there were Atwater blood in those veins.

Lupe, her black hair cascading around her shoulders, brought me a Dos Equis without asking.

"Good to see you, Fitz," she purred, pulling a notepad and stubby pencil from the apron hung around her ample hips. "What will it be this evening, gentlemen?"
Poole finally raised his scummy head. "I don't need nothing to eat. And this beer's on him."
"Very good, sir," Lupe raised her eyebrows at me. "What about you, Fitz?"

"Just a couple enchiladas, Lupe, and beans."

" *¿En caso de que mi padre tiene su bate de béisbol listo? Este chico se parece a un verdadero imbécil."* Lupe asked as she wrote down my order. I understood what she was asking: my short air force career in Texas left me with a decent understanding of Spanish: "Should my father have his baseball bat ready? This guy looks like a real jerk."

"I don't think so, but thanks for asking," I answered.

Lupe walked away, smiling at me over her shoulder.

"What did she say? I hate fucking wetbacks who don't talk good English when they come to this goddamn country."

"She just wondered if I wanted to see the dessert tray."

"Hers?"

"I'm here to ask about where you were the night Gina died."

"I was in Akron, at my sister's. We were celebrating my daughter's birthday. I told the fucking cops this shit."

"You got proof?"

Poole reached inside his jacket and pulled out his phone. With a few clicks, he showed me a picture of himself in a pink tiara, smiling at a little girl in a similar pink tiara. There was a birthday cake with five candles, surrounded by ashtrays with burning cigarettes and beer cans in front of the pair. At the corner of the shot, someone's tattooed knuckles spelling the word KILL, held a beer mug. In the background, long beards and big guts in tattered tee shirts filled the shot. No other faces were visible. The photo was time-stamped in the opposite corner, just after nine-thirty Saturday night, half an hour before Gina's time of death.

Good times. Holy shit. I nodded and Poole put his phone back inside his jacket.

If he truly was in Akron and the time stamp was accurate, he was at least forty-five minutes away when she died. I made a note to have Ambrosi subpoena Poole's phone and have the data analyzed—hopefully, the photo would have a location map embedded as well as a time stamp. Even if he deleted it, any good forensic lab would be able to recover it.

"I assume you know how she paid the bills," I said.

"Yeah."

"What did she do?" Poole had to know she was a hooker, didn't he?

"The system doesn't make it easy for anybody on the dole."

"That's the idea. The system is designed to make you go out and get a job."

"Or work around it."

" So you know she had sex with other men for money."

Poole shrugged. I got a sick feeling in the pit of my stomach.

"She whored for you, didn't she? You're her pimp." He leaned back in the booth and smirked.

"There are a lot of things I asked Gina to do. That wasn't one of them."

" Like what?"

"Mr. Fitzhugh, or whoever the fuck you are, the man who killed my daughter's mother is in jail."

"And he says he didn't do it. I'm obligated to provide information for his defense that proves that."

"So you're looking to run my ass into the ground to get that weasel dick Atwater off? I got proof. I didn't kill her."

"You want to give me the address of that birthday party? Names of some of your fine associates?"

Poole rattled off the names and phone numbers of everyone at the birthday party as I scrawled them into my notebook, all of them known members of Road Anarchy. He signaled for another beer as Lupe brought my plate. I laid my pencil down and picked up a fork.

"Did you know she had door locks installed on the outside of the kids' bedrooms?"

Poole arched an eyebrow.

"You're comfortable with your daughter being locked in her bedroom in case of a fire?"

"I didn't say I was."

"I'm hearing stories of a cop who harassed Gina for sex. Know anything about that?"

Poole took a drink of his new beer and shook his head.

"I know a cop was leaning on her pretty hard. She didn't say what it was about."

"Could it have been in regard to anything you're doing?"

Poole put the beer bottle down slowly.

"What's that supposed to mean?"

"Exactly what I said. Are you involved in something that could have gotten Gina killed? You tell me you didn't kill her yourself, but I know your record, Poole. You're no angel."

Poole's eyes hardened. "Michael Atwater is in jail for killing Gina. I think that says everything." He took another sip from the beer bottle and stood up. "If you need anything else, I think you need to talk to my attorney." With a smirk, Poole strolled toward the door. Tossing a twenty on the table, I jumped up and followed him out into the late day sunshine.

"Poole!" I said. "I'm watching you."

He whirled around, stepping close to me with clenched fists. I could smell the beer on his breath.

"You trail me and you'll regret it."

"If you haven't done anything illegal, you don't have anything to worry about."

Poole flipped me the bird and walked away. He got on a big black Harley Davidson Fat Boy parked about halfway down the block, fired up the bike and roared down the street.

Then I saw him from the corner of my eye—the man who'd been watching me from the town square.

He was leaning against the wall of Lupe's place, wearing sunglasses and the same black ball cap low on his forehead. The collar of his black leather jacket was pulled up to further obscure his meaty, pockmarked face.

He tried to turn and walk away unnoticed but I grabbed him by his jacket collar, shoving him against the dirty bricks.

" Who the fuck are you? Why are you following me?" I punctuated each question with a shove, sending his thick skull against the bricks. "Answer me, motherfucker! Answer me!"

He shoved me away and ran toward the alley. I followed, my legs pumping like pistons. Within a few steps, I was close—close enough to grab him in one horse-collar move. As I grabbed his shoulders, his feet flew out from under him and he landed hard on his back between my feet on the dirty gravel, blinking. I stood above him and pulled out my Glock.

"*Who are you?* Answer me or I'll blow your head off!"

He started to reach inside his jacket. I offed the safety. He froze.

"Tell me who the *fuck* you are and why the *hell* you were watching my office! *Now.*"

"My name is Jorge Rivera. Who I work for isn't important." His was the same rasping voice I'd heard when I'd been cold-cocked outside my office.

"Bullshit. Why are you watching me?"

"You need to leave this case alone."

"What if I won't?" I stepped back and Rivera scrambled to his feet, grabbing his cap. I kept my Glock leveled at his face.

"Gina Cantolini didn't die for the reasons you think. Don't mess with something that's bigger than you, Fitzhugh."

"Bigger than me? How?"

"It just is. Be smart—leave it alone. Just leave it alone."

"I need more than just your warning. I got too many people telling me something more is going on and a man in jail for a murder I'm convinced he didn't commit."

Rivera shifted nervously from one foot to another. "I can't."

"Why not?"

"Because they'll kill me."

"Who's 'they'?"

Rivera didn't answer. He turned quickly and ran down the alley.

"Hey!" I shoved my Glock back in my shoulder holster and followed. Rivera was faster this time; I couldn't keep up. He turned down another alleyway and I lost sight of him.

I made it to the corner when a single shot, muffled by what had to be some kind of silencer, rang out. Someone moaned and I heard the thump of a body hitting the ground. I threw myself against the side of a building and pulled out my Glock.

Carefully, I leaned around the corner, weapon ready, expecting to see Rivera dead on the ground. Nothing—nothing but trashcans. And silence. I stepped tentatively into the alley, taking cover wherever I could, searching for Rivera.

By the time I made it back into the light of the street, I was flabbergasted.

Where was the body? Who shot him? And why?

Chapter 6

No gunshot victims showed up at Fawcettville General Hospital.

I checked.

The sour, middle-aged woman in happy face scrubs at the emergency room desk looked at me over her glasses.

"Why do you need to know?" she asked.

"I was chasing a man down an alley. He turned the corner and I heard a gun shot. When I turned the corner, he was gone—or what was left of him."

"And you don't think the staff here wouldn't call the police if a gunshot victim showed up?"

"I didn't say that."

"If we had a gunshot victim here, this place would be crawling with cops. Do you see any cops here now?"

"No."

She rolled her eyes like I was the dumbest asshole she'd seen all day. Maybe I was, but it wasn't worth my time to explain my case or myself to her. I walked out the door.

I didn't expect Rivera—or what was left of him—to show up, but I had to ask. If he made it to Akron, or Steubenville alive, I'd be surprised. If he were dead, whoever shot him would most likely dump the body on a slag heap at some abandoned steel mill, where it wouldn't be found until the skeleton was picked bare.

I returned to my office to think over everything I'd found out.

Mac Brewster wouldn't talk to me until he'd submitted his retirement papers—but what he wanted to tell me probably led more into the floundering marriage that was infecting Chief Monroe's professional career. Brewster was too much of a Boy Scout to kill a fly, much less some drunk whore.

I pulled out my notebook and dialed one of the phone numbers Poole gave me.

"This you, Fitzhugh? Poole told me you'd be calling." Charlie Horton was one of Road Anarchy's officers and one of my frequent flyers when I was a cop: plenty of drug abuse, mostly fighting and some auto theft. It was his tattooed knuckles I saw in Poole's cell phone photo.

"Yeah, Charlie, it's me. I need you to come down to my office and talk to me about the birthday party Jacob Poole had for his daughter Saturday night."

"You still a cop?"

"Nope, I'm a PI now. Michael Atwater's attorney hired me to do some investigation."

"Then I don't have to do shit, do I?"

"We can always issue a subpoena and depose you."

"Go ahead."

"So was the cake good?"

"Yeah. It was. You know me, Fitz. I love little girls—and their birthday parties." Charlie hung up. I wanted to vomit.

So, if Charlie was to be believed, Jacob Poole was at his sister's house, in a room full of goons, sharing birthday cake with the daughter he'd had with Gina. The time stamp on the photo proved he didn't kill Gina, even if he wasn't in Akron.

I made a note to tell Ambrosi.

Atwater admitted he argued with the victim over her requesting a DNA test, but said his wounds came from a drunken fall, a story that was thin at best. As much as Ambrosi wanted to believe his client was innocent, I still wasn't buying it.

I wasn't being paid to believe in someone. I was being paid to do a job. I needed to talk to Reno Elliot.

*****

It was two in the morning when I opened the door at Puccini's coffee shop. The long-haired college student, his ponytail corralled in a hair net, looked up from whatever book he was reading and stood up from his seat near the cash register.

The place still looked like a hangout for teenaged girls in poodle skirts, who babbled about Bobby Darin. The red and white striped awning over the front window matched each booth's upholstery lining up on the other side of the glass. The stools at the counter were patent leather red. Next to the cash register was a display case where rows of Joe Pucca's famous Italian pastries sat, waiting to be purchased: *pizzelles*, *biscotti,* Italian doughnuts called *bomboloni* and *ciarduna siciliani,* tiny sweet cookie shells filled with mascarpone or ricotta cheese. Inside the case, a sheet of paper clung to the glass with yellow, cracked adhesive tape: "WE DO WEDDING CAKES" was written in fading ink. A huge brass espresso machine, the same one I'd operated as a teenager, sat on the other side of the counter, surrounded by tiny white espresso cups and saucers, bottles of flavored syrup at attention along the mirror behind it.

The only nod to this century was the electronic cash register and the industrial strength coffee machine.

I sat down at the counter and ordered a decaf and a cannoli.

"So, I'm looking for a cop named Elliot. He works nights. Does he come here at all?" I asked when the kid brought my order.

"Big black guy? Bald? Maybe mid-thirties?"

"That would be him. He come in tonight?"

"Not tonight. I overheard him talking last week about going to see family someplace."

I nodded and took a sip of decaf. And maybe he's on the run from a murder.

"He's popular though."

"How's that?"

"You're the second person tonight who's been in looking for him."

"That so? Who else was looking for him?"

"Some Latino guy in a jacket and black baseball cap."

"What? What time did he come in?" Rivera was here? He couldn't have been—he'd been shot. I'd heard it myself. Unless… Rivera had done the shooting and he'd been the one to drag the body off. If that's the case, who is this latest victim?

"The Latino guy—he come here often?"

The kid shrugged. "Maybe a couple times a week. He and the cop would sit over there and have a cup of coffee." He pointed at a booth in the corner, one that gave customers a good view of the sidewalk without being seen.

"What did they talk about?"

"I never paid attention. They didn't argue though. Neither of them ever got loud at any rate. I figured he was an undercover cop or something. They'd talk for maybe half an hour, and then they'd leave, but never at the same time. They were good tippers."

"Did they come in about the same time every week?"

The kid thought a little bit before he answered. "Yeah, kinda. They'd come in anywhere between two and three thirty, usually. Cops on nights get lunch breaks, right? I figured they were on lunch break."

"Thanks." I took a bite of my cannoli and the kid walked back to his seat beside the cash register. When I finished, I paid my bill and got back in the Excursion.

As I drove through Fawcettville's dark streets, some of this shit was starting to fit together. The same thug who was tailing me knew the crooked cop and met with him on a regular basis. That same cop, Reno Elliot, had to be intimidating Gina Cantolini.

Maybe he even killed her. That would explain why nobody wanted me looking into the case, why it would just be easier to let Atwater hang for her murder. Monroe had too many strikes against him—if he had a crooked cop on the force, it would be just one more reason why the city manager would can his ass. If he had a cop who killed a hooker, it was even worse.

Maybe what Mac Brewster had to tell me was more than just the long sad tale of Chief Nathaniel Monroe ruining his professional career. Maybe I should sit down with him again and listen to what he had to say.

But that still didn't explain what made Gina a target.

Maybe it was nothing more than covering up the actions of a bad cop to save Chief Monroe's ass. If his position with the city was as precarious as Brewster told me, and he knew he had a bad apple in his basket, along with a sleazy wife in his bed, it could spell the end of his time at the helm of the FPD.

I smiled as I drove. What I wouldn't give to be the one to push Chief Monroe out the door.

I stopped the Excursion at the intersection and realized where I was. Three houses down on the right was the Tudor I'd shared with Grace. I'd unconsciously driven back home.

As I pulled up to the curb, a soft light shone from the front bedroom. I knew it was the light on the nightstand beside the brass bed. Gracie was a notorious night owl. She probably couldn't sleep again and was probably reading or grading papers from her music theory class.

At least I assumed she was. Maybe she wasn't alone. Maybe Van Hoven was up there with her. Maybe she wasn't grading papers.

I sat behind the wheel, chewing my thumbnail.

I met Gracie when money went missing from the college music department and the college hired me to do the quiet digging before calling in the cops.

Asked by the college president to interview each member of the department, I stood outside her office door, letting the warm sounds of her cello fill the hallway before I knocked.

The tall beauty answered the door and took my breath away. Long, slim fingers of one hand held her cello's neck and the bow as she reached out to shake my hand with the other. A loose skirt showed off thin hips and her black curly hair hung around a white boat necked blouse.

Her dark eyes met mine, shooting something I'd never felt deep into my gut, and I couldn't speak.

"Well, you're either the oldest student I ever had request lessons or you're the private dick that everybody is bitching about," she said.

"I'm—I'm the—the," I stammered. This didn't happen to a wop like me. I was the one who could coax the panties off any woman in record time. I didn't stand in anyone's doorway at a loss for words, but now, here I was, dumb as a boy at his first middle school dance.

"You're the dick. I get it. Come in. Let's get this over with."

The interview went well, not that the beautiful Dr. Darcy was ever a suspect. Eventually, the department secretary, a little old lady who verged on terminal virginity and whose eyes got large as saucers every time I entered the department offices, admitted to forging department checks when her trips to the Wheeling, West Virginia casinos didn't go as planned. She paid everything back and quietly retired at the end of the academic year. No charges were ever filed.

Meanwhile Dr. Grace Darcy and I met every day for lunch on the college commons. We had dinner at her Tudor style house in the hills after symphony rehearsals and nights… Dear God, the nights. I closed my eyes, as if that could keep away the pain of what I'd lost.

I was truly the frog who'd been kissed by the princess, although our marriage didn't lead to any magic transformation on my part. Simultaneously elegant and rough-edged, the Julliard and Yale-educated doctor of philosophy and the troll-like son of a steel town beat cop were the odd couple at faculty events, the subject of gossip at the symphony, but we didn't care. We were happy.

Gracie opened up worlds to me I never would have experienced without her. There were performances with other small symphonies around the country and music education conferences across the globe. She dragged me to Eisenach and Leipzig, Germany one summer to teach me about Johann Sebastian Bach. She taught me about legendary cellists Casals, Rostropovich and Yo-Yo Ma; I taught her how to shoot a beer can off a fence post. I still remember her delighted squeal when she hit one dead on.

I knew this frog married a princess when, just before our wedding, we spent Christmas at her folks place in Greenwich, Connecticut.

Her dour, reserved family lived in a ritzy stone house that would encompass four blocks of small, New Tivoli clapboard houses.

"Jesus Christ," I said as the wrought iron gates opened and Gracie drove our rented Toyota up the circular brick driveway.

"Yeah, it isn't much but it's home," Gracie said ruefully. "This place, the condo in St. Thomas and the place in Aspen."

"You're fucking kidding me, right?"

"Nope." She shook her head. "My father was a heart surgeon and Mother can claim a direct line back to the Pilgrims."

I whistled low as we stepped from the car and I lifted our suitcase from the back seat. I was entering a world I knew nothing about. We'd passed estate after palatial estate on our way from the airport and the air got more rarified.

This was not the place a dago mick like myself was likely to be seen—or welcomed. Thirty years ago, I would have been intimidated by the high price lifestyle. Then again, thirty years ago, I never would have landed anybody as classy as Grace Darcy.

"And before we go in the door, I need you to know that my parents always felt very disappointed that I didn't marry a hedge fund manager and become the Junior League stay-at-home social princess with two-point-four spoiled brats. They also don't consider me a 'real' doctor and have equally as many disappointments about my brother."

"What horrible things did he do?"

"Got addicted to heroin, robbed a convenience store and spent four years behind bars in his twenties."

"I can see how an academic life teaching college students to play the cello would be a horrible burden for a parent to bear, Dr. Darcy." I slipped my arm around her waist. Gracie smiled and kissed me.

"My brother was a violinist," she continued as we walked across the brick driveway to the wide double doors. "After prison, he started a music program for at-risk inner city youth. While I was at Juilliard, I spent summers teaching cello to some of them. I decided I wanted to teach after he died of an overdose a few years later."

"Even at some provincial college in a has-been Ohio steel town?"

"Especially in a has-been Ohio steel town."

After dinner, we stood in Darcy's dark parlor, decorated extravagantly for the holiday, holding sterling silver cups of eggnog spiked with Chivas in front of a roaring fire.

"What exactly does our daughter see in you, Mr. Fitzhugh?" Mrs. Darcy asked.

"I'm not sure," I said. "I just know she loves me and that's enough for me."

Mrs. Darcy—she never asked me to call her anything but Mrs. Darcy—twisted her pearls and pursed her lips. Leaning on the mahogany mantle, Dr. Darcy looked over his half-glasses at me but didn't speak. We never went back.

Yeah, Gracie was a catch on a lot of different levels.

And, after six years, it was ruined.

If I went to the door and knocked, would she let me in? Would she curse me for coming by at this ungodly hour? Or, if she was alone, would she open the door and welcome me in? Into her arms—or her bed?
Probably not, judging from the conversation we had the other day.

Maybe that Van Hoven asshole was there, just as I imagined, even though there were no strange cars in the driveway. Maybe he really was in her bed, where I should be.

Maybe she was right. Maybe I should sign the papers and we should move on.

I put the Excursion back in gear and drove back to the office.

Chapter 7

By nine in the morning, I was back at Puccini's coffee shop, this time meeting over espresso with the Italian Festival organizers, a group of older civic-minded Tivoli Gardens' residents, most of them retired steel workers, their spouses or widows.

The Italian Festival started in the fifties, before I was born, by a group of World War II veterans in conjunction with the local Sons of Italy Lodge as a bocce ball tournament at the city park. Over the years, the bocce ball tournament died off and the event became a downtown celebration of Italian food and wine with local bands thrown in.

It was Sophia Armando, this year's festival committee president, who discovered Gina Cantolini's body. At least seventy five, she dyed her coiffed hair jet black, wore heavy black eyeliner with fake Bambi eyelashes and bright red lipstick, trying to retain the beauty she once had as a young woman. She and her husband, Eddie, had a boat up on Lake Erie, so her clothing seldom lacked some sort of nautical print.

She was sharp as a tack and no one you wanted to mess with. I learned that when I brought her daughter, Barbara, home late from a high school dance. That hadn't changed. Sophia ran the Italian Festival committee like she ran her home: toe her line or find something else to do.

She tapped her fake red nails against the white espresso cup in front of her.

"Niccolo, how is your mother?" she asked as I slid into the only empty chair at the table of six. "I haven't seen her in a couple weeks."

"She's fine, Mrs. Armando, she's fine."

"I made a big pot of pasta fagioli—too much for Eddie and me. I'll take some to her later this afternoon."

"That would be kind of you."

"So I thought they caught the boy that killed Gina Cantolini." An older man, one I didn't recognize, spoke up.

"They arrested someone, a guy named Michael Atwater," I said. "He's been charged, but his attorney believes he's innocent and hired me to look into what happened that night. That's why I asked you all to meet me."

Sophia shook her head and shivered. "I've never seen anything like that, Niccolo, never in my life. That poor girl!"

"Did any of you see her before she was killed?"

"She was arguing with a man, a redheaded guy. He was pretty drunk. I was selling raffle tickets at the festival information booth and saw them both."

"There was a policeman working at one of the booths," someone else interjected. "He was handing out information. He stepped in and broke it up."

"That black kid? Officer Elliot? He's such a nice young man." Sophia thoughtfully tapped her chin with a sharp red nail.

"He broke up a fight between the victim and a redheaded man?" I pulled a notebook from inside my hooded sweatshirt. "An actual physical fight or an argument?"

"It was an argument, but a loud one, very, very profane. Completely inappropriate for a family festival," Sophia said, shaking her head. "I got the feeling that one of them was going to hit the other if it wasn't stopped. And people around them were scared."

"So Officer Elliot stepped in? Was he in uniform? Was he on duty?"

"Officer Elliot was off duty, but he had his uniform on, since he was working the police department booth, right next to the festival information booth. He stepped in between them and got them to go their separate directions."

"Did they?"

"Yes. The redheaded man walked about three blocks and I didn't see him after that. He was really drunk."

"You didn't see him fall down at any point?"

Sophia shrugged. "No."

That wasn't good. Atwater claimed his injuries weren't from physical contact with the victim, but from a fall. Maybe I'd have to convince Ambrosi our boy was guilty after all.

"Anything else stand out about the whole situation?"

"Not really." Sophia knit her black-penciled brows and took a sip of her espresso. "No wait—Officer Elliot said something really odd after he came back to the booth."

"What was that?"

"He called them both a 'waste of humanity who don't deserve to walk this earth.' I thought that was a little harsh."

Truth be told, Gina Cantolini *was* a waste of humanity, but she didn't deserve to die like that—and Michael Atwater was an asshole but he didn't deserve to go to jail for a murder he didn't commit. Maybe Atwater didn't do it, just like Ambrosi thought.

My money was still on Reno Elliot. He was looking more and more like the bad cop who could be capable of killing a hooker.

And if that resulted in Monroe losing his job, it was all I could ever want—besides winning back Gracie. And hell, if I got both my wishes, I'd be on top of the world.

I just needed to find out everything I could about Elliot.

I put my notebook inside my coat and finished off my nearly cold espresso.

"OK, thanks."

"Tell your mother I'll be over later this afternoon with the soup."

"Will do."

I got Barnes on the cellphone while I drove. I had some time before I was supposed to meet with Ambrosi and fill him in on what I'd learned so far.

"Tell me about Reno Elliot."

"Shit, Fitz. I told you everything I knew the other day. He's the boyfriend of one of the assistant prosecutors, the blonde one named Alicia. For the life of me, I can't ever remember her last name. Linnerman? Lonnergan? Hell, I don't know. Anyway, Elliot played football for KSU, like you, only he didn't get thrown off the team. He's only been on the force for about a year or so."

I ignored the jab. "How many departments has he worked for?"

"What do I look like, HR? Call 'em yourself and ask."

As a private citizen, I'd have to go through the chief with a public records request to get into Elliot's personnel file and I knew Chief Monroe would stonewall me for as long as he possibly could. I'd have to make some calls, do some digging on my own.

"Is he off this week?"

"How should I know?"

"One more question—you know anybody named Jorge Rivera?"

"Nope. Why?"

"Just curious."

"I know you better, Fitz."

"Yes, you do. Thanks, Barnes. Talk to you later."

Before I got to Ambrosi's, I stopped back at the office, to call guys I knew on other departments from around northeast Ohio. They told me everything I needed to know: Elliot was young and arrogant and had all the makings of one hell of a bad cop. He'd been through four departments in the ten years he'd been in law enforcement. He couldn't—or wouldn't—follow orders, had more than one complaint of excessive force filed and was investigated several times for discharging his weapon, once into the tires of a car belonging to the teenage son of a county commissioner. There was some talk—none of it proven—that he'd filched cash from the evidence room on more than one occasion. He managed to resign and move on before anything could be pinned on him.

The first couple times, the union stood behind him on most disciplinary actions, but that didn't surprise me any. That he was able to keep getting jobs did.

Somewhere along the line, he hooked up with Alicia Linnerman, an up and coming young lawyer now working for Dennis Lance, the county prosecutor. She'd been there just under a year and somehow managed to get her boyfriend on the FPD.

Why is it sharp, educated women like Alicia Linnerman always fall for wrong guys like Reno Elliot? Maybe Gracie could give me the answer.

Then again, maybe Alicia wasn't as sharp as I thought. Maybe she was one of those desperate females who were thrilled any man paid any attention to her. In my mind, I envisioned Alicia as a tall, thin TV lawyer in an expensive suit and heels, giving the jury an aggressive, bulletproof opening statement that would convince jurors of a defendant's guilt before the first witness took the stand. Maybe she wasn't.

Suddenly the tall TV lawyer morphed into the short, slightly overweight woman, who lived alone with three cats and binge-watched Netflix most weekends while stuffing her fat face with Cheetos. In this new assumed portrait, Linnerman's courtroom techniques would have been OK, but not flamboyant. Maybe she accepted Reno Elliot's offer of a date because she believed down deep in her heart that no one else would ever find her interesting.

Maybe she wasn't "up and coming." Maybe she would be one of those young lawyers who'd stay an assistant prosecutor for her entire career, a female version of Ambrosi. Small towns were full of them.

The clock in the waiting room chimed. I changed into the blue sport jacket that was hanging over a chair by my desk. I needed to get over to Ambrosi's office and fill him in.

*****

Ambrosi's office was as dull and as gray as he was, only he had enough business to pay for a secretary to answer the phone. Despite the three sad sacks sitting in the waiting room, she led me back to Ambrosi's office as soon as I walked in the door.

Ambrosi's office stunk from the cheap cigar he clenched in his yellow teeth. He stood up to shake my hand.

"What happened to your face?" he asked.

"Some goon was trying to make a point. I'll tell you later."

"So what have you found out?"

Quickly, I filled him in on my interview with Susan Atwater, Mac Brewster and the kid at Puccini's. I finished with Sophia's story about the argument.

"I think that Reno Elliot has some real possibilities. He could be the real suspect, given that he's been heard asking the victim for sex and calling her a waste of humanity. But he said something to the kid at Puccini's about going on vacation this week. I don't think I can talk to him."

"Maybe you can." Ambrosi pushed today's issue of the Fawcettville *Times* my way. Reno Elliot's picture was splashed across the top of the page: *FPD officer held on sex assault charges in Akron.*

Chapter 8

Elliot was picked up in Akron after a half-dressed woman, bleeding from facial wounds, ran screaming from a cheap motel into the street where a passing cruiser rescued her, according to the story.
The officer made an attempt to flee in his vehicle; a short chase ended when he hit a parked car six blocks away. He had scratches on his face and arms, and was carrying his badge.

The report from the Akron police department identified their suspect as Reno Elliot. The paper didn't have a mug shot but instead ran his FPD shot from the department web site. It was hard to reconcile the picture of the smiling cop sitting in front of the American flag with what I knew.

The victim was a known drug addict and prostitute with an extensive record; Elliot met her at the corner and allegedly beat her after sex. She suffered facial fractures and two broken ribs, the story said.

I looked over at Ambrosi.

"This doesn't look good for Elliot, but it looks good for our case," I said.

"You think Elliot killed Gina?" he asked.

"I think there's too many things which could tie him to the murder at least circumstantially." I filled him in on what I'd found out. "He's got a checkered career at best and now he's been arrested for beating the shit out of some working girl."

"We'll be stirring up a hornet's nest if we accuse a cop of murder. You know that, don't you?" Ambrosi didn't look like he had the backbone.

"What are you afraid of?" I asked. "If you're too afraid to do what it takes to get your client off, you don't need to be in this business."

Ambrosi squirmed.

"Or is this why you're paying me? Because you haven't got the balls?"

"You don't think Jacob Poole has anything to do with this?" Ambrosi asked.

"I'm not sure. He showed me a picture on his phone. He said he was at a birthday party for his daughter, supposedly at his sister's house. I also spoke to Charlie Horton, a member of Road Anarchy. He said he was at the birthday party, but wouldn't come in to talk to me. If I were you, I'd subpoena the photo and depose Charlie Horton as fast as I could. I'd see if somebody could find where that photo was taken and if the time stamp is accurate. If it turns out that Charlie's telling the truth and the photo is accurate, then Poole is off the hook."

"So what happened to your face?"

I filled him in on Rivera, including the shooting in the alley, his alleged post-mortem appearance at Puccini's coffee shop, along with his previous acquaintance with Elliot.

"What does he have to do with this case?"

"Maybe a lot, maybe nothing at all. I think that the word went out from the jail straight to Chief Monroe that I was investigating this case. Monroe's out to get me—he has been for a long time."

"Over what?"

"It's a long story—one that doesn't make either of us look very good. Anyway, I think Monroe heard I'm on the case and he panicked. Everybody knows Chief Monroe is wrapped up with who his wife is doing on a daily basis. Half the folks on the force would love to see Monroe lose his job. And if it's over a dirty cop, especially one who commits murder, so much the better."

"Ah yes. Mrs. Monroe. I've heard quite a bit about her. Not a good situation for a man like the Chief."

I grimaced.

"I'm betting he thinks Rivera's intimidation will shake me off the case."

Ambrosi exhaled the smoke from his acrid cigar toward the ceiling and nodded. I couldn't tell if he was worried about casting aspersions or if he'd suddenly developed a spine.

"You need to talk to Reno Elliot, especially if we want to present evidence to clear my client."

*****

Elliot was being held at the East Crosier Street Jail in Akron, about an hour from Fawcettville. Males and females were held in the five interconnected diamond-shaped pods surrounded by razor wire and a neighborhood that had seen better days. Because he was a cop, Elliot was being held in isolation for his own protection.

He sat across from me in the visiting bay, separated by bulletproof glass.

He looked like he'd had the shit beat out of him. His angular brown face had long fingernail scratches down each cheek. There were abrasions on his muscular arms and on the side of his shaved head. His knuckles were bloody.

I wondered how much of the damage came from the hooker and how much of it came from the crash and his apprehension.

If he hadn't been so roughed up, I guess I could have seen how someone—Alicia Linnerman, for example—might even think he was handsome.

We picked up the receivers to talk.

"Who the fuck are you?" he asked.

"They didn't tell you my name before they brought me back here?"

"Yeah. I don't know any Nick Fitzhugh."

"I'm a PI. I'm looking into what happened to Gina Cantolini and your name keeps coming up."

"How's that?" His lip curled sarcastically.

"You broke up a fight between the victim and her boyfriend Saturday night at the Italian Festival."

"So?"

"You were also heard demanding a blow job from the victim before she died."

Elliot smirked but didn't answer.

"Another thing, Officer Elliot, I'm a retired cop. One thing I and my other law enforcement brothers and sisters don't take too kindly to is assholes like you who tarnish the badge."

Reno leaned into the glass, his fist tightly clutching the phone receiver that linked us.

"Listen, I don't know why you are here and frankly I don't care—"

"I'm here because I've put some things together about you—and they could make you a pretty likely murder suspect. I know what kind of cop you are. I know you've bounced from department to department because you're either too stupid to do what you're told or you're one of those arrogant dicks who thinks a gun and a badge is a license to break all the rules." I leaned in closer, too. I knew the conversation was being recorded and I wanted the jailers to catch every word. "I think this girl who got away from you wasn't your first. I think you like hitting women, particularly powerless ones who won't or can't fight back. I think you found a sad drunk whore in Gina Cantolini and you made her your target."

I waited for him to say something, but he didn't, so I kept going.

"You think you have a built-in alibi for the night she died when you were seen breaking up a fight between her and Atwater, but you were overheard giving your opinion on their worthiness to walk this earth. Atwater may be an asshole and a loser, too, but he's got as much right to oxygen as Gina did."

Elliot leaned back slightly, but his expression didn't change.

"I think you wanted something from the victim and you went looking for her that night. Only this time, what you wanted from her was something she got tired of giving you and she fought back. When she fought back, it pissed you off, like it does anytime someone stands up to you, just like the working girl here. So you killed her—you choked her when she wouldn't shut up and then you shot her. To cover your tracks, you dumped her body back at the festival, where enough people saw her arguing with Michael Atwater to hang him for the crime."

Elliot leaned back toward the glass.

"You think you can make that stick? Talk to my lawyer."

"And could that lawyer be Alicia Linnerman? You got her conned, too, Reno? You hit on her?"

"You keep Alicia out of this."

"The only thing I haven't got figured out about this whole thing is where you did it. And I'm not going to stop until I do."

Elliot slammed the received down and called for a guard to escort him back to his cell.

*****

Back in Fawcettville, I stopped at the prosecutor's office, which was on the second floor of the county courthouse. The courthouse was across the street from the Civil War monument in the center of town, a block from my office, a big Romanesque limestone building, each of the three public entrances flanked with a pair of Neptune statues staring blankly at those who came through the door.

The prosecutor's office entrance faced the white marble staircase that led upstairs to the courtrooms. I stepped through the door. The spring sunshine shone through a pair of arched stained glass windows, shining blue, green and purple hues down on a row of clerical workers, kept from the public by a rail and gate moved there from the last courtroom remodel.

Dennis Lance, the prosecutor, had an office to the left of the entrance, behind a big carved mahogany door. I knew from experience the four assistant prosecutors had individual cubicles in the office to the right of the entrance.

A large wooden frame showing a pyramid of each staff member's photo hung on the door above their names, which were engraved on brass plaques. Lance's "Look at me, I'm your next judge" face was at the top of the heap. Alicia Linnerman's photo started at the next row.

Her face wasn't what I thought she'd be: she was neither the tall, gorgeous, TV lawyer in expensive suits, nor the lonely, overweight woman desperate for a man, but a plain-faced competent-looking blonde with glasses and a welcoming smile.

I pointed at the photo.

"I want to see her."

"I'm sorry, Miss Linnerman is in meetings for the remainder of the afternoon," the secretary said.

"It's four-thirty. Thirty minutes isn't long. I'll wait till she comes out," I said, seating myself.

"The meetings aren't here," she said firmly. "They're off site."

I stood up and pulled a business card from my sweatshirt pocket. "Got it. Please tell her I stopped by."

"Will do, Mr. Fitzhugh," she said accepting my card.

Back outside the courthouse, I leaned against one of the majestic maples on the courthouse lawn, watching the employee entrance. At five o'clock, right on schedule, a female matching Alicia Linnerman's photo came out the secured door and walked to her car.

"Off-site" my ass.

I got a good look at her as followed at a safe distance. She may have had bad taste in men, but she didn't look at all like the lonely cat lady I'd first imagined. She was medium height, a little plump, but in a good way; she was wearing a pair of outsized sunglasses, and a very lawyerly navy suit.

Parking wasn't easy in downtown Fawcettville—most everyone coming to the courthouse, including the employees, had to find a spot in the adjacent lot. Only the judges and other elected officials were lucky enough to have designated curbside parking. Lucky for me, Alicia Linnerman's car was parked just one row over from my Excursion. Even luckier, her bright yellow Volkswagen Beetle made it easy to follow her through what passed for rush hour traffic.

I followed Alicia to her home. She lived in the only swank apartment complex in the hills overlooking Fawcettville, a complex where the muckety-mucks and wannabes lived before they decided to move on to bigger things or put down money on a house.

I parked on the street and watched which apartment she went into before sprinting up the sidewalk and knocking on her door.

She threw the door open, smiling like she was expecting someone else, holding a glass of white wine in her hand. A big grey mastiff ran out from the back of the apartment growling. I reached inside my hoodie, making sure I could touch the Glock in my shoulder holster.

"Down, Sadie, down!" Alicia ordered, her smile gone. The mastiff sat obediently. "May I help you?" I pulled my hand from inside my jacket and handed her a business card.

"Miss Linnerman? I'm Nick Fitzhugh. I'm a private investigator. I need to ask you a few questions about Reno Elliot. May I come in?"

"Sure. Is this about the incident in Akron, or... something else?"

I followed her into the living room, furnished in sleek hipster grey and lime furniture.

"Something else, sort of."

"Mr. Elliot and I are no longer romantically involved, no matter what he or his attorney might have told you."

"I'm investigating the murder of Gina Cantolini. Her body was found Saturday night under the stage at the

Italian Festival. I'm working for the defendant's attorney, Jim Ambrosi."

"I know the case. I'm not handling it, but if I were, I'd have to tell you to talk to Mr. Lance about it. I can't give you anything, especially not here."

"I just need to ask a few questions. Were you working at the festival when Officer Elliot broke up the fight between the victim and the defendant? I talked to festival organizers earlier and they said a female was working the police department booth Saturday when the fight occurred." *No they hadn't, but she didn't need to know that.*

"Yes, I was. I was handing out neighborhood watch information. Officer Elliot did break up a fight—I saw that."

"What time was that fight?"

Alicia shrugged and took a sip of her wine. "The middle of the afternoon— two, three o'clock maybe? The man, who I later learned was Mr. Atwater, was pretty drunk."

"After Officer Elliot broke up the fight, my client says he fell and injured himself. Did you see him fall?"

"No."

"And after that happened, how long did you work at the police booth?"

"Couple hours, then I went home."

"Did Officer Elliot go with you? Was Officer Elliot with you all Saturday night?"

"You're not looking at him as a suspect in the Cantolini murder are you?" Her directness took me by surprise.

"I have some information that points to him as a potential suspect, yes."

"He was here, with me." She looked a little uncomfortable.

If you're going to be a lawyer, you'd better develop a better poker face than that.

"You understand, then, when I ask if anyone else was here to verify that?"

"There were others here, yes."

"Who?"

Alicia sat her wine glass down on a glass-topped table. She pulled up the sleeve of her blouse, exposing her upper arm, which was marred with blue finger-shaped bruises.

"As you know from the incident in Akron, Reno has some issues—with women and with anger. Saturday night he accused me of sleeping with my boss, Dennis Lance, then tried to beat the shit out of me. My neighbors and half the Fawcettville police force were here."

Chapter 9

"So you're saying that Reno Elliot couldn't possibly be Gina Cantolini's killer because at the time of her death, he was beating you up?"

Alicia Linnerman was no shrinking violet—and from the size of Sadie, no crazy cat lady either. She looked me straight in the eye and nodded.

"He tried to at any rate. He grabbed me by the arm, as you can see, and slapped me a couple times, but Sadie put an end to that real quick—she had him cornered in the bathroom by the time the police responded. Didn't you, girl?" Alicia pulled her sleeve back down and patted the panting mastiff on the head. "I'm too nearsighted to be a good shot, so as a woman living alone, Sadie is the next best thing. She proved that Sunday night. Elliot was taken in and charged with misdemeanor domestic violence, but they let him go, ROR."

"Released on his own recognizance." I nodded. "I'm surprised that didn't show up in the paper."

Alicia shrugged. "I can't comment on how the police do or do not handle press inquiries on one of their own. There's an awful lot of ugly going on at the FPD right now. I'm sure you could get a copy of the report, though."

I sighed. "If they filed one. I don't believe, and Jim Ambrosi doesn't believe, that his client Michael Atwater is guilty. I hoped I was onto something with Reno Elliot, but I guess not."

"I hate to disappoint you, Mr. Fitzhugh. I'd like to hang the bastard as much as you would, but I think a murder charge won't stick." Alicia picked up her glass of wine and walked toward the kitchen. "Can I get you something to drink? A glass of wine? A beer? It might take the sting off a bit."

"Call me Fitz," I said, following her into a small kitchen that was just as trendy as the living room. "Sure. A beer sounds great."

Alicia opened the fridge and leaned over to pull a beer from the bottom shelf. I liked the look of her round behind, still in the conservative navy work skirt she'd had on when she walked out of the courthouse.

She stood quickly, catching my stare and blushed as she handed me the beer. She pulled a pilsner glass from a cabinet and sat it on the kitchen table, across from her wine glass.

"Have a seat, Fitz. Tell me about yourself."

I twisted the cap off the beer bottle.

"What do you want to know?" I turned to toss the bottle cap into the trashcan behind me. "Or should I ask, what have you heard?"

Alicia smiled and took a sip from her wine.

"A couple friends over in domestic court that mentioned you one or two times. I know you do a lot of work for the divorce lawyers in town."

I nodded. "That's true. I retired from the police force about seven years ago and got my PI license. It pays the rent."

She looked down at her wine glass and spun it between her fingers. She looked up over her spectacles. Her eyes were cornflower blue, ringed with thick black lashes and sucked me in with their intensity.

"You married?"

"I'm separated."

"Ahhh."

"What's that mean?"

She smiled and shrugged. "Just asking."

"So let me ask you a question. How'd you end up in Fawcettville? And with Reno Elliot?"

Her smile turned a little sad. "I came to Fawcettville basically so I could be a big fish in a small pond, maybe make my name on a big case or two. As for my personal life, I was just out of Cleveland Marshall College of Law and tired of working in Akron when I met Reno on a case."

"As a defendant or as a witness for the state?" I took a sip of my beer. I liked this girl. I liked her a lot. Why did she get involved with a scumbag like Elliot?

"Aren't you snarky? I was in the prosecutor's office then, too. So he was a witness, when I met him, of course," she said. "I wasn't aware of his background then and over the last year as I learned more about him, defended him to everyone I knew, like anybody involved with a jerk does."

"Was this the first time he hit you?"

"He was never the calmest guy I ever dated. But in the last six months or so, I saw a lot more anger—I don't know why. We had more arguments and they escalated pretty quickly. Before Sunday, I never understood that dynamic with the DV cases I'd handled. Let's just say I've become a little more sympathetic."

"I'll bet."

"Mind if I ask why you and your wife separated?" She looked at me again with those fierce, cornflower blue eyes.

"It was a bit of a compromising situation. Let's just say that."

"I've heard that about you, too." Her eyes didn't move from my face. She may have just split up with a boyfriend, but this girl wasn't letting any grass grow under her feet. I shifted uncomfortably in my chair.

"I was always faithful to my wife, OK?"

"I thought you said you were caught in a compromising position."

"It wasn't what it looked like, but unfortunately I can't convince her of that."

"I understand." She didn't look like she believed me.

We were silent for a moment as each of us sipped our drinks, both trying to figure out what hung in the air was between us, whether it was going to stay professional or veer dangerously, for me anyway, into the personal. It was probably best to change the subject.

"I hear your boss is thinking about running for office."

"Yes. He wants to be the next Common Pleas judge."

"Think he'll be a good one?"

She took a sip of her wine before she answered.

"I think he'll be pretty good. Dennis is a good guy."

"That sounds pretty non-committal. I always liked working with him when I was with the PD. You know something I don't know?"

She shrugged and smiled.

"We're kind of getting roped into campaigning for him—unofficially of course. He hasn't got anyone running against him yet but he's bought us all tickets to some big thing this weekend."

"The symphony benefit?"

"Yes. He's aware of current ethics laws, so anyone who didn't want to go didn't have to. Everyone in the office has rented tuxedos and we'll be wearing campaign tee shirts with them: 'Lance for Judge' or something like that."

"My wife plays cello for the symphony. Her name's Grace Darcy, Dr. Grace Darcy. She teaches music theory at the college—and cello, of course."

"Oh? So will you be there?" The blue eyes drilled through me again.

"Yes I will. Grace is performing." It was time to go. I stood, drained my bottle and sat the empty on the counter. "I want to thank you for your time, and the beer. I'm sorry for what happened to you, but it clears Officer Elliot of murder."

The predatory vibe emanating from her side of the table seemed to diminish. She tossed back what was left of her wine and escorted me to the front door. Sadie jumped off the couch as we passed and, once at the door, stood beside me, pawing my leg. I reached down and scratched her ear.

"She doesn't do that with just anybody," Alicia said. "You must be a nice guy, down deep inside."

"It's the same story—all I attract is dogs and dangerous women." I smiled.

Alicia laughed. "And all I fall for is bad boys."

I leaned in close, close enough to smell the wine on her breath and sense the heat of her skin. I wanted to kiss her, the first time I'd felt that way in a long time. She tipped her chin up; I cupped it with my hand, leaning in for the kiss.

I stopped. I couldn't do it—not if I wanted to get Gracie back.

"And despite what Sadie believes," I whispered. "I'd be just another bad boy."

She stepped back and smiled as she opened the door. "That's too bad, Fitz. I get the feeling you might just be worth the trouble."

*****

Back at my office, I sat the cardboard tray holding my fast food dinner on the desk and flopped into my chair. I opened the lower desk drawer and sighed, pulling out my wedding picture from the bottom drawer, where it lived next to its neighbor, the bottle of bourbon.

I held the wooden frame in both hands. We'd gotten married at city hall by the judge. Gracie was wearing an off-white dress that stopped at her knees and a small veil; she carried a bright red bouquet of roses. Her snooty parents didn't attend. I wore my best navy blue suit. My mother took the picture of the two of us standing in front of the smiling judge.

Saturday night was the symphony benefit and an event we'd made into a standing date. It generally followed a standard theme: beginning with a cocktail hour, then moving to dinner at themed tables extravagantly decorated by a group of symphony spouses. Following dinner, there was an auction of items donated by area businesses, then the symphony performed.

If you were in business or in politics, it was a great place for recognition and meeting with your constituents, as Dennis Lance obviously had planned. Anyone who thought they were anything usually attended, along with long-time symphony supporters and music school faculty from the college.

I took my paper dinner napkin and wiped a smear from the glass covering the photo. Gracie and I were a fixture there. Now that we were separated, why did I even decide to go? Would Gracie even acknowledge me there? Could I stand to see her next to Van Hoven all evening?

By the time I'd met Gracie and decided to settle down, the horn dogging I'd done was a thing of the past. Or had Maris Monroe just scared the shit out of me?

Back then I had an apartment in one of the old converted Victorians in New Tivoli, six blocks from my newly widowed mother.

I'd met Maris once or twice for drinks after my shift. I knew I was playing with fire, but I didn't care. It was all about the hunt, the conquest of easy prey, not about getting back at my boss for anything although, down deep, if I thought about it, that was probably why I was really going after his wife.

I didn't like Nathaniel Monroe when he was assistant chief and I disliked him even more when he made chief. He got conceited and big headed when he pinned on the chief's badge. He treated the officers below him like dirt and the rank and file's opinion went downhill even faster when he dumped his long suffering first wife and took up with Maris.

Like I said, I wasn't the first notch on Maris Monroe's bedpost; I was just the first to get caught. She and I found carnal delights for six nights in a row on most of the solid surfaces at my place before everything blew up.

We were on the kitchen floor. She was on top of me when the chief pounded on the door. My hands were exploring the luscious contents of the pink lacy bra bursting out of her shirt as she straddled me; her matching panties were on the floor beside us.

"Open the door, Fitzhugh!" he screamed. "I know you're in there, and I know my wife is with you!"

"Oh my God! Oh my God! He must have followed me here!" Maris jumped up and began buttoning her shirt.

"The door, Fitzhugh! Open the fucking door!" The pounding got louder; it sounded like he was using the butt of his gun. "Maris, I hear you in there! Maris!"

"What do I do? What do I do?" She quickly zipped her skirt and slipped into her shoes.

"Here—" My kitchen window faced the back alley; I opened it and helped her outside onto the fire escape, tossing her purse to the ground as she ran down the iron stairs.

The hinges on the door gave, splintering the doorframe as Chief Monroe burst in, his weapon drawn. Behind him, my neighbor, the elderly Mrs. Falletti, standing in the hallway in her white muumuu and pink sponge rollers, screamed.

"Where's my wife? I know she's in here!" Monroe shoved the barrel of his gun in my face.

I held up my hands. With a quick kick, I tried to send Maris's underpants beneath the fridge, but Monroe was faster. Keeping the gun trained on me, he bent down and grabbed the pink panties with his free hand.

"Who do these belong to, Fitzhugh? Your sister?"
"So I fucked your wife. I'm not the only one. Go ahead—shoot me. Nobody would blame you," I said. "You can spin the story however you like. You'll make certain you come out looking like the hero, I'm sure."

In the hallway, Mrs. Falletti gasped.

Monroe grabbed me by my shirt and jammed the gun barrel beneath my jaw. I lowered my hands, but didn't try to resist. Twenty years on the force just went down the shitter. So why be afraid to die? My mother would grieve, as would my brothers and sisters, but the manner of my death wouldn't surprise anyone. Hell, they probably would think I had it coming.

"Let go of him!" Mrs. Falletti cried. "Don't shoot him!"

"Here's how it's going to go, Fitz," he hissed into my ear. "You've been stalking my wife. You conned her into meeting you for drinks—yes, I know she met you every night this week—and then you abducted her. I followed her phone's GPS signal here to your apartment, we struggled, and I shot you in self defense as my wife escaped."

He pulled back the trigger and I closed my eyes. I was going to die over a goddamned piece of ass.

Footsteps pounded up the stairs. Three cops, with their weapons drawn, burst into my apartment. One of them was Lt. Baker.

"Drop the gun, Monroe! Drop it right now!" he commanded, his service revolver trained on the chief. Monroe lowered his weapon and released me.

"We know what happened here, Nate. Your wife just called me," Baker continued, sharply. "If you shoot Fitz, you're done as a cop. You will spend the rest of your life in prison and you'll ruin the reputation of this entire police force. You want to ruin your career over some cheap broad like Maris? It's easier to get divorced."

Monroe stepped back and holstered his weapon, glaring at Baker. He turned to me.

"You got lucky, Fitzhugh. I had every right to blow your brains all over this wall. I want you in my office at ten thirty tomorrow morning. There will be disciplinary action."

Monroe and the two other cops left the apartment. Baker waited until the door downstairs closed to speak.

"You're a good cop, Fitz, even though you've pulled a lot of stupid personal shit over the years. I want your retirement papers on my desk half an hour before you're supposed to meet with Monroe. You're not going to that meeting with him. This is for your own good and you know it."

Within six weeks, thanks to some pals at the Bureau of Criminal Investigation, I had my PI license and six months later, I met Gracie.

Had I learned my lesson with Maris Monroe or had I been lucky enough to meet the love of my life? I never could decide which one it was.

I traced Gracie's face on the photo with my finger. Even though I might not be able to nail Reno Elliot with Gina Cantolini's murder, I would find out who really killed Gina Cantolini. The big question was if I could get Gracie back.

Chapter 10

I woke up stiff and sore on my waiting room couch Friday before the sun came up. I folded up my blanket and put it, along with my lumpy pillow, in the waiting room closet, sighing as I wondered how many more uncomfortable nights there would be on that cracked leather beast.

My dying marriage needed to go on the back burner for now, however. I needed to focus on nailing Jacob Poole. Pinning Gina's death on him was my last hope to free Michael Atwater. Was there something in Poole's life that could connect him to Gina's murder? I hoped so.

My cell phone beeped with a text message as I filled up the coffee pot in my office bathroom.

It was Ambrosi. He'd subpoenaed Poole's phone at my request. Yesterday, Poole (and his attorney) willingly showed up, turned over the phone and the tech people Ambrosi hired were looking into it.

Not the actions of a killer.

Maybe I shouldn't waste time looking into the actions of a man who was cooperating fully with the investigation, then. But where should I turn?

Reno Elliot didn't kill Gina. His demands on her were pretty fucked up and he was one shitty cop, but the bruises on Alicia Linnerman's arm proved he wasn't around to kill Gina.

But who was Jorge Rivera and what was his relationship with Elliot? Who shot him—or whom did he shoot? And where was the body? Was Rivera tied to

Monroe somehow? Who hired Rivera to push me off the case and why?

I sipped my coffee as I flipped through the Atwater file, going through the same basic facts one more time. Nothing jumped out at me. Nothing.

There were steps outside my office door and today's newspaper slid through the mail slot. I shuffled over to pick it up.

Two lead stories screamed for attention above the fold. On the left was a story about Gina's funeral, slated for this afternoon: "Murder victim to be laid to rest." On the right were Dennis Lance's head shot and the story "Prosecutor seeks Common Pleas bench."

Maybe I ought to look into Gina Cantolini—maybe her past could lead me to a reason for her death. I scanned the story, which was basically a recap of the murder. Oddly enough, no next of kin was quoted or named.

Why wasn't her family mentioned? Maybe my answers lay there.

Her parents didn't live here, according to stuff she'd told me when I'd arrested her in the waning days of my police career.

She was just eighteen and already a drunk, with the sad face of someone much older and much more defeated than someone three times her age. I picked her up trying to shoplift a bottle of whiskey.

"You got family to come get you?" I asked, trying to meet her sodden eyes in the cruiser's rearview mirror. "They'll book you and then release you since it's a misdemeanor."

"No." She wouldn't return my gaze. Instead, she watched the traffic go by, leaning her forehead on the window.

"Nobody?"

She didn't answer.

"Where do you live?"

"On the street. Sometimes I stay at the women's shelter at the United Methodist Church."

What a sad, sad story, I thought at the time. Wasn't there someone, somewhere who cared for this kid?

Now, seven years later she was dead and I couldn't find out why.

Growing up, I couldn't recall anyone named Cantolini in the New Tivoli neighborhood, but that didn't mean anything. Like any kid, my world existed only in the three-block area where I was allowed to ride my bike. There could have been multiple Cantolini families living cheek by jowl in the duplexes that marked the edge of New Tivoli two blocks over—I would have never known. No one from my high school class had that moniker, but again, I didn't know if that was a married or a maiden name. For all I know, Gina could have been born a Smith, a Jones, or a Johnson.

I had a week before the grand jury convened. I needed to get busy or Michael Atwater would be facing a murder trial. I needed to consult my ultimate source on New Tivoli. I picked up my cell phone and punched in a number. In a few rings, she picked up.

"Ma? Hey, it's me, Niccolo. No, no. I'm fine. No, there's no crisis. Yes, Gracie is fine. No, I haven't moved back home yet. I'm calling early because I wanted to catch you before you went to Mass. I need to ask you something about a case. Can I come over later this morning? Is after Mass better? I'll see you then."

*****

The white house I grew up in sat on a small corner lot, circled by Ma's Floribunda roses. Since Dad's death a few years ago, she'd thrown herself into gardening, replacing the tulips, the marigolds and the petunias with the same roses she carried on her wedding day. Using Dad's life insurance money, she'd had the clapboard exterior covered in aluminum siding, since he wouldn't be around to paint it every five years, but left the interior of the house stuck in the mid-seventies.

I knocked, bracing for how she'd look when she came to the door. Ma was always thin, but these days had shrunken to a bird-like ninety-five pounds, her dowager's hump stealing more and more of what little height she had left. She pinned her gray hair in the same tight bun she'd worn the day Officer Aidan Fitzhugh pulled her over for a broken taillight in 1949. I knew I wouldn't have Maria Gallione Fitzhugh in my life much longer; her appearance at the front door of that white house reminded me every time I saw her.

Today was no different. She still had her black dress on from this morning's mass, but she'd taken off her orthopedic shoes and replaced them with pink fuzzy slippers.

"Niccolo! Niccolo!" Sounding like she'd just gotten off the boat from the Old Country, instead of being a lifelong Fawcettville resident, she reached up to hug me then waved me inside. "Come inside! Come inside!"

I shut the oak door behind us and followed her through the dark living room and into the kitchen. A pot of *pasta fagioli* simmered on the old, olive green stove.

"I see Sophia Armando brought you some soup," I said, taking a seat at the familiar dinner table.

"And it tasted like *merda.* This is fresh." Ma spit into the stainless steel sink with disgust. "Sophia Armando is the worst cook in the neighborhood. I threw hers out as soon as I tasted it. Why did you tell her she could bring that *immondizia* to my house? Coffee?"

I shrugged. There was never any sense in arguing with Ma, no matter what the subject. "Sure."

She put a tiny cup of espresso in front of me and I loaded it up with sugar. I waited to speak until she shuffled over with her own cup and sat down across from me. Maybe I shouldn't have.

"So when are you and Gracie getting back together?" she demanded. Her claw-like hand trembled slightly as she lifted her cup to her lips, her eyebrows arched.

"I don't know, Ma."

"What do you mean you don't know?" She stopped sipping, gesturing widely with her hands.

"I didn't come here to talk about Gracie."

"What do you mean you didn't come here to talk about your wife? What kind of husband are you? I get twenty grandchildren from your brothers and sisters, but the one son I tell everyone is my favorite, the one who follows in his father's footsteps, God rest his soul, I get *niente*, nothing."

"Ma."

"That's what happens when you decide you gotta wait until you're old enough to be a grandfather yourself before you get married—"

"Ma, I'm not old enough to be a grandfather."

"Sure you are! Sophia Armando's daughter, remember her? The one you dated in high school? She got married right out of nursing school and had four children before Sophia was fifty-five, the same age you are now. Thank God, you didn't marry Barbara though. She probably couldn't cook any better than her mother. Not that I would have tried to teach her—that's a mother's job to teach their daughters how to cook. I wouldn't have shared my marinara recipe with her anyway. She would ruin it."

"Ma! Stop it!"

"What do you want, then?" Ma looked at me like I was being rude. Her white espresso cup clinked delicately on its saucer as she sat it down.

"I came here to ask you if there were ever any Cantolini's that lived in the neighborhood."

"Cantolini? Hmmm..." She tapped her index finger on the table. "There was one family, down near Puccini's, but they moved away by the time you were in eighth grade. They had a son, I think, and a daughter. You wouldn't have known them because the kids, they went to St. Rita's. I wanted you kids should have a good Catholic education, too, but with us living on a cop's salary, that wasn't possible. So we sent you to the city schools. That wasn't too bad. I mean, you got a football scholarship out of it, didn't you?"

"Focus, Ma, *focus*. Where did they move to?"

Ma shrugged. "How should I know?"

"I'm trying to find information on the family of that girl who was murdered. Think, Ma. These folks could have been the victim's grandparents. If you can just give me a name, it's something to start with."

"Let me see... The parent's first names, they started with A, I think." Ma rested her chin on her hand, thankfully silent for the moment. "Anselmo? No, that's not it. Adalberto? No. Wait! *Alberto!* That's it! Alberto! The father was Alberto and the mother was Luisa. They came here after the war. The son's name was Brian and the daughter's name was Ava. There!" She threw her hands up in the air triumphantly. I reached across the table and clasped her grey head in my hands, kissing her forehead.

"Thanks Ma," I said sinking back into my chair. "What can I do to repay you?"

"Your brothers all married idiots. You were the only one to marry a woman with brains, the only daughter-in-law I can hold a halfway decent conversation with. Go home and make things right with your wife. That's all I ask."

*****

Gina's funeral was held at one of the less classy funeral homes at the edge of Tubman Gardens. Susan Atwater was sitting with her two grandsons in the front row, dabbing at her eyes. Prosecutor Dennis Lance was sitting at the other end of the same row. After today's newspaper story, I didn't know if this was to assure the attendees of the hard work his office would do to convict her killer or if it had morphed into a campaign stop.

A small group of Fawcettville's rougher residents walked through, paying their respects to Gina's two boys and nodding at Susan Atwater. A few sat in the back rows, intending to stay for the service.

When I was a cop, I spent a lot of time with these folks. These were the people who rode on Fawcettville's ragged edge, both legally and socially, men and women who worked with their hands and didn't use gloves, who woke up on Saturday morning hung over and without their weekly wages, if they had any to start with. Their clothes were stained and their steel-toed boots mud-caked, their faces lined with the cost and the dirt of their lives. Uneducated, unwashed and uncouth, even for a dago mick like me, they would throw punches or shank someone at the first perceived slight. Many, like the Atwaters, were the hardscrabble Appalachians who came to Fawcettville to work in the potteries and the mills; they brought with them their mountain fierceness, hard drinking and clan loyalty.

For whatever reason, they adopted Gina.

I got in line to pay my respects to the deceased. Gina's face was plastered with pasty makeup, and a silk scarf tied around her neck to hide the strangulation marks. I wondered how much work the undertaker had to do to repair the bullet wound in her chest.

Susan Atwater left her grieving grandsons to stand beside me.

"Such a sad, sad story," I said softly. "Does she have any family here?"

Susan shook her head. "Just the kids."

I took her elbow and steered her away from the casket and the line of mourners.

"I'm still working to free your son," I whispered. "I found out the cop didn't do it."

"You're sure?" Susan's long bony fingers picked at her sleeve.

"I'm sure. He was beating up his girlfriend at the same time Gina was killed, so he couldn't have done it. I need to ask you a couple questions."

Susan sighed.

"Who claimed the body? Who paid for this funeral?"

"I identified the body and found the funeral home. The bar where Gina worked took up a collection to pay for this. They came up with about half, but then supposedly some anonymous donor paid the rest."

"What do you mean 'supposedly'?"

Susan shrugged. "One of the folks from the bar told me he thought it was the prosecutor. Said he heard it from someone who worked for the funeral home."

"No prosecutor in his right mind would do that—for ethical reasons, if nothing else. Did you ask him if it was true?"

"I'm not asking that bastard *anything*," she hissed. "He wants to kill my boy! He wants the death penalty! I can't believe he had the nerve to even show up here."

Canned organ music began to play through the speakers in the ceiling; my conversation with Susan ended as mourners began to take their seats. A preacher I didn't recognize—not that I knew who the priest was at St. Rita's, either—got up to lead the service. My thoughts raced, and I barely listened as the service droned on.

Could the rumor be right? Why would Dennis Lance pay for the funeral? Why would the prosecutor help pay for a murder victims funeral, if it wasn't to curry votes? How ethical could that be, especially in light of his formal declaration as a judge candidate? Probably not very ethical at all, considering he'd already declared he wanted to see Michael Atwater face the death penalty. An action like that, if it were true, would kill any conviction on appeal —or at least I would think it would. I'd have to ask Ambrosi. My opinion of Dennis Lance was changing and not for the good. Susan Atwater had to be wrong— *had* to be. If not, I had to ask what was going on in this town? Between Chief Monroe and the prosecutor, had everybody's ethics gone down the shitter?

I stood as six mourners, in black T-shirts and jeans, walked Gina's now-closed casket down the aisle and out to the hearse. Slowly, the crowd shuffled out, a few of them stopping to hug Gina's boys or shake Susan's hand. A few stopped to talk to Lance; he made sure to look properly concerned and sincere, as any good candidate would. As the last of the mourners filed out, he approached Susan, his hand extended, looking like he was mining for more votes. Without a word, she turned on the worn heel of her shoe and, grabbing the boys by the hand, walked out.

Chapter 11

It was Saturday morning and I was sitting at Lupe's Mexican restaurant, enjoying huevos rancheros and searching the Internet on my laptop.

Lupe came by and draped her arm around my shoulders. She leaned over me to pour another cup of her strong coffee.

"Qué estás haciendo?" she asked, sliding into the booth beside me. "What are you doing?"

"Working a case," I said, squinting at the screen. I needed reading glasses, but was too vain to go get them. It would mean I'd have to admit I was middle aged. Ma's comments that I was old enough to be someone's grandfather didn't help. *Fuck this getting old shit.* "I'm looking into my murder victim's past."

I hadn't found much, except Alberto and Luisa's death records in Pennsylvania, where Alberto found work with U.S. Steel. Both died in Pittsburgh about the time Gina would have been in kindergarten. The trick was finding out where the hell their children went —and whether Gina was Brian's daughter or Ava's.

Most of what I needed—death and birth certificates, divorce or marriage records—I could order online, but Michael Atwater only had a week before the grand jury convened and I couldn't wait for the mailman to solve my case.

Driving the ninety minutes to Pittsburgh to see Alberto and Luisa's old neighborhood might or might not have gotten me the information I needed. People in their age group were probably already dead or retired to Florida. There might not be anyone around who knew them.

My chances were a little better with the Internet and any court records I could dig up. Hopefully they would be in the surrounding counties. Nearly every county around here was considerate enough to archive every damned piece of paper connected to recent court cases, from original appearances, to media requests to have cameras in the courtroom, verdicts and sentencing hearings. All I needed was to find what I needed, then click the 'download' button and I was good to go. The catch could be if the court records went back further than twenty years. If they were, they'd be archived someplace, maybe offsite, away from the courthouse, which could cause additional delays. I'd have to drive to the courthouse to pick up the documents—more wasted time.

"If you need anything else, *cariño*, you just call," Lupe said, sliding out of my booth, and running her hand familiarly along my shoulders.

I waved absently as she left. I was running out of time and needed to find something to jumpstart this case, not the sweet, warm smell of a woman.

Using my index fingers, I typed "Ava Cantolini + Ohio" into the computer, hoping for enough of a news record to start my search. I hit paydirt: the results located an Ava Cantolini outside of Cleveland in Shaker Heights. I flipped through a few newspaper entries: She married a businessman named Jones, hyphenated her last name and was active in all the right social climbing crap. She organized the bake sales at her children's private school, was active in the Junior League and even had an exhibit of her photography at a local gallery. All Shaker Heights references of her stopped, then picked up a couple years later with another photography exhibit in San Francisco.

That's a hell of a long way to move. Why leave Ohio? Was this the right Ava Cantolini-Jones? A little further down I got my confirmation with Alberto's obituary: "... He is survived by his wife of 67 years, Luisa, and a daughter, Ava Cantolini-Jones (Sam) of San Francisco, six grandchildren, Louis, Lena, James and Jennifer Cantolini-

Jones, and Gina and Mariella Cantolini. A son, Brian, preceded him in death. Services will be held…"

So Gina was Brian's daughter, huh? Looks like we're making progress, I thought as I took a sip of my cooling coffee. I punched in "Brian Cantolini + Ohio" and my jaw dropped.

Four pages of archived newspaper stories filled my screen: "Local teacher charged with sex crimes," "Jury hears graphic testimony in teacher sex-crime case," and finally, "Teacher charged with sex abuse commits suicide."

The news stories in the *Akron Beacon-Journal* were ten years old. I would have been near the end of my police career and too wrapped up in my own life to pay attention to anything that happened out of town; Gina would have been fifteen.

When I picked her up seven years ago for shoplifting, she was eighteen and already had a drinking problem, and probably a drug problem as well. Maybe her problems started when Daddy Brian thought he'd visit her bedroom late at night. Maybe that bastard was the one who started her down her destructive road. Maybe getting to know Gina a little better, even post-mortem, might lead me to her killer.

I skimmed one of the stories: Brian had been a beloved English teacher at one of Akron's most elite private schools, introducing his students to Whitman, Keats, and Shakespeare. Then his wife, Sharon filed for divorce—along with a Department of Family Services complaint that Brian had sexually abused their daughter. The school administration was notified, which triggered a long and loud school board meeting, filled with acrimonious comments by supporters on both sides. Brian's suspension, along with his vehement denials, was front-page news and so was the trial.

A few more clicks and I found video from an Akron TV station. The reporter stood outside the Summit County courthouse, interviewing a black-haired man in a trench coat. The crawl at the bottom of the screen said it was Brian Cantolini.

He had the same kind of John Wayne Gacy face I'd seen thousands of times before: a little plump and starting to sag with age. His beady eyes didn't match the warm and welcoming smile. I could see where his supporters thought he was just a great English teacher, who opened their child's minds to the mystery of poetry, and encouraged their love of literature and writing.

As a cop, I knew better.

Brian Cantolini was the same kind of guy who showed up at kid's parties as a clown, luring young boys and girls over to his house where he'd offer them toys and candy and games and, when they were comfortable enough, made his move to destroy their innocence, their psyches and fuck up their entire lives.

No wonder Gina was a drunk at 18 and dead by 25. "This whole thing is a vendetta engineered by my ex-wife," Cantolini told the reporter. "I never did what she accused me of. I never laid a hand on my daughter!"

The reporter leaned in to ask another question, but Brian's lawyer held up his hand.

"We will not try this case in the court of public opinion," the lawyer said. "Our case will show that these charges are completely fabricated, engineered to ruin a good man and keep a great teacher from doing what he does best."

I clicked the video off. *Whatever.* That's what all those perverts said. At least I knew where Gina went off the tracks.

I clicked through a few other stories: apparently, Gina's recorded testimony was shown in closed court; the graphic nature of Brian's deeds caused one juror to vomit and another to leave crying, according to the story.

Two days later, before Brian even had a chance to present his defense, he blew his brains out.

At least he saved the State of Ohio a lot of money on appeals and prisoner meals.

I clicked back to Ava Cantolini-Jones. Her move to San Francisco looked like it happened about the same time as Brian's suicide, no doubt out of shame and embarrassment. Can't blame her—living with the knowledge that your own brother was a pervert and abused your niece must be a bitch.

I pulled a ten-dollar bill out of my wallet, tucked it under my coffee cup and stood, folding my laptop under my arm. Lupe, taking someone's order at the back of the restaurant, waved as I left.

I wonder where Sharon Cantolini was these days? Maybe she could help me find out some more information. Like why she didn't show up at Gina's funeral?

Or pay for it?

Those questions weren't appropriate for Lupe's place on a Saturday morning. Besides, it would take a little longer to chase her down and I needed to get ready for the symphony benefit.

After I left Lupe's, I got a haircut and a shave at the barber's down the street from my office. My tuxedo was hanging in the waiting room closet for me—and I should have been thinking about Gracie—but I had a few hours to kill before I slipped into the monkey suit and begged my wife for forgiveness.

I wanted to find Sharon Cantolini first. I plugged in the laptop again and started searching for phone numbers. No luck, at least in Ohio. I went back to the Summit County Clerk of Courts web site and began looking there. Nothing—at least she kept her nose clean after Brian's suicide.

Maybe she tied the knot again? I searched the Probate Court records for a marriage license. *Boom!* There it was: Sharon Cantolini got remarried a year after Brian's suicide to some schmuck named Joe Hansen, a loan officer at a local bank. At the time of her remarriage, she was living at an address in North Canton. Out of curiosity, I jumped back to the Auditor's web site and checked the property tax records, just to see how—or if—the widow

Cantolini spent her soon-to-be ex-husband's life insurance money.

The house was in a neighborhood of older well-kept homes, built in the 1920s, along a group of streets named after Ivy League colleges. The house, at the corner of Northwest Princeton and East Yale streets, was nothing extravagant, nothing suspicious, well kept in a genteel, upper class sort of way, judging from the photo. She bought the house eight months after Brian's death. After she tied the knot with Joe Hansen, his name was added to the deed and hers was changed to reflect their nuptials.

A few more clicks and I had a home number. *Thank God for those of us who still have landlines.* I punched the number into my office phone and waited for Sharon Hansen to pick up the phone.

A perky "Hi, you've reached the Hansen's" was the only voice I heard on the other end of the line. Oh, well. I left my name and number and the reason for my call. Hopefully, she'd call me back.

Maybe there were reasons why she didn't come to Gina's funeral. Maybe Brian's abuse just caused too much damage and Sharon lost touch as her daughter fell into her destructive lifestyle. Maybe Sharon didn't know Gina was dead—or that she had three grandchildren. Maybe Sharon was in ill health and couldn't come. Maybe she was too ashamed of the life her daughter had adopted—or maybe just too judgmental. Families put up walls over the damnedest things.

Who knows?

At any rate, what mother wouldn't want to help in the search for her daughter's killer?

Chapter 12

If I were back at home, I would have spent this Saturday on the couch, watching a baseball game, drinking a beer with Gracie at my side. I wouldn't worry about this shit until Monday. Living at the office made it hard to stop working.

Maybe a little distraction would help me out. I wandered over to the television atop the filing cabinets across from my desk and turned it on. I leaned back in my office chair and put my feet on the desk. I pulled the remote from the middle desk drawer, flipping through the infomercials and old movies, settling mindlessly on some blonde trying to sell cookware.

Within a few minutes, the phone rang. I leaned over to pick up it up, leaving my feet on the desk.

"Fitzhugh Investigations."

"Mr. Fitzhugh? This is Sharon Hansen." Her voice was mouse-like and timid.

I sat up straight.

"Hello! Thanks for calling me back, especially on a Saturday. I'm sorry to bother you at such a bad time, but I'm investigating the death of your daughter Gina and just had a couple questions."

She sighed. I hated talking to victim's family members. This one could be especially hard. The woman had lived through the sexual abuse of her daughter by her husband for God's sake. Now that daughter, who obviously struggled with keeping the horror of her abuse at bay through drugs and alcohol, had been murdered.

"What do you need to know?"

"I'm looking for information on Gina, her background and any contact you might have had with her recently."

Another painful sigh.

"Gina and I have been estranged for a number of years. Her drug and alcohol problems were so severe that I had to separate myself from her. I'm sure you understand." The words caught in the back of Sharon's throat. How much agony did this woman have to endure?

I'd seen enough addiction and concerned family members to know that, sadly, happened sometimes. The violence, the theft, and the drama: after a while you just had to shut the door for your own self-preservation. But her daughter was dead. The drama —with her at least—was over. She deserved a decent goodbye.

"I saw the stories in the *Beacon-Journal.* You and your family have been through a lot. I hate to see something like that happen. But I have to ask why you didn't come to her funeral?"

"I've been in ill health for some time, Mr. Fitzhugh, and confined to a wheelchair. I can't drive anymore as a result, and I couldn't find anyone to bring me."

"I'm sorry to hear that. It was a nice service."

Sharon was silent.

"So are you aware you have three grandchildren?"

"No, I'm not." Her mousy, pained voice turned flat.

That's an odd reaction. Most people I know would be thrilled to know they're grandparents. Not me, of course, but then I'm not most people.

"Two boys and a girl. Cute kids."

"Mmm."

"I heard that the bar Gina worked at raised money for her burial and got about half the amount. Some unknown benefactor paid for the rest, supposedly. Do you have any idea who would do that?"

"No I don't. As I told you, Mr. Fitzhugh, I've been out of touch with my daughter for a number of years as a result of her addictions. It's been a long hard road. I'm sorry I can't help you."

"You don't want to know what's going to happen to your grandchildren? Or what is going on with the investigation?"

"I'm sorry. It's not that I don't want to help, it's just that I can't." She hung up.

That's weird.

What about Ava? Maybe Ava Cantolini-Jones had a little more insight into this mess. I turned the laptop back on and began my search again for phone numbers. The Indians were playing the Tigers by this time and losing by a run. Maybe by the end of my phone calls, they'd be ahead.

I didn't find any "Ava Cantolini-Jones" and no "Ava Cantolini" listed by herself, so I made the assumption Ava and her husband Sam were still married.

I started with every Sam Jones listed in San Francisco; when that didn't work, I tried every "S. and A. Jones" listed, then every "S. Jones." After hours of hearing "Sorry, wrong number" my blood pressure was up and the Indians were down another run. *OK, one last try and I fucking quit.* I pushed in the number for the last S. Jones and listened to the phone ring.

In the background, the announcer droned on: *It's the bottom of the ninth and there's two outs. Indians are up to bat. They trail by two runs and the bases are loaded—*

A young boy, his voice cracking with puberty, answered the phone. "Hello?"

There's the wind up—

"Hi, I'm looking for Ava Cantolini-Jones?"

And the pitch—

"Hang on." The phone made a *thunk* as he dropped it. I heard a yell: "Mo-o-o-om! Pho-o-o-one!" I held my breath as footsteps came closer to the phone. *Please let them belong to the woman I'm looking for.*

In the background, the announcer kept talking. *He swings—*

"Hello, this is Ava Cantolini-Jones."

He connects with a powerful crack of the bat and that ball is flying! It's on fire!

"Hi, my name's Niccolo Fitzhugh. I'm a private detective. I'm looking into the death of Gina Cantolini."

"She's dead? I didn't know that. That breaks my heart." She sighed.

And the ball sails up, up, up—it's heading toward the scoreboard—

"Yes ma'am. She was murdered last week. They found her body under the stage at the Italian Festival in Fawcettville. I was wondering if you can tell me anything about her, specifically, her mother Sharon."

"Oh, I can fill you in on Sharon."

And it's a goner! It's a home run! The Indians win!

"What can you tell me about her? Anything specific you think would help my case? I'm looking into—"

"That bitch? It's about time somebody exposed what she did to my brother." Ava turned from a well-bred California mom back to her hardscrabble eastern Ohio roots.

"Excuse me?"

"Sharon fabricated everything she had that girl say on the stand. Nothing that girl said was true! Nothing! That little bitch ruined a good man and I tell you from the bottom of my heart, my brother never did that! Never!"

"Wait a minute! Wait a minute! You mean Gina? It was Gina who testified against her father, right?" I couldn't believe what I was hearing. I pulled the TV remote from my middle-desk drawer, shut off the post-game celebration and put Ava on speaker. I needed to hear every nuance in her words. Her rage and the anger burned through phone lines, and she was near tears. This had been simmering for a long, long time.

"No, Gina didn't testify against her father—she was the only one in that family who wasn't bent on destroying Brian! It was Mariella, the older one."

I thought back to Alberto's death notice.

"Mariella was a younger sister? She was listed second in your father's obituary, behind Gina."

"Mariella is five years older than Gina. She was twenty when Sharon and my brother split up."

"She was twenty when she accused her father of sexually abusing her? What the hell started that?"

"Sharon manipulated her into doing it. She called her at night at her college dorm—Mariella was going to Akron State, and wasn't happy there. Sharon started unloading on Mariella about how miserable she was being married to her father and somehow planted the idea she'd caught her father abusing her when she was a little girl."

"What?"

"Sharon was a master manipulator. I never understood what Brian saw in her, but he was a bookworm, never dated much. He probably thought that some babe like Sharon was going to be his dream girl. She wasn't." Ava spit out the word like it was poison.

"What was Sharon like?"

"She was horrible to live with. She put on one face for the public, where everyone thought she was sweet and lovely and did no wrong, but she was different behind closed doors. Brian told me after the girls were born he couldn't do anything to make her happy. He'd do anything that woman wanted. If she wanted a new car, he'd get her one, even on a teacher's salary. She wants a new house? They go looking for one. Sharon always dressed to the nines—she never went out without looking like a million bucks. Once, on a whim, she wanted their bedroom painted, so my brother takes a whole Saturday and paints those walls the color she wanted and everything. And when she got home with the girls from a shopping trip, she told him it didn't turn out the way she wanted and to paint it back the original color. And he did it!"

"Wow."

"So she keeps working on Mariella, feeding her this garbage that Brian abused her, all the while riding him like a rented mule. He was too fat; they didn't live in a nice enough neighborhood, why hadn't they gone to Europe like all her fancy friends? He used to call me on his way home from work and tell me all this crap. He was miserable and then he finally met somebody, somebody who treated him like a human being. It was one of the other teachers where he worked. When he realized he didn't have to be this unhappy, Brian starting thinking about filing for divorce. He couldn't stand Sharon anymore."

"What happened then?"

"Brian didn't understand why Mariella suddenly wouldn't talk to him, so he took a day off from work and drove up to see her at college. I always thought Mariella was a lot like her dad, really gullible and in some ways not real bright, but she had her mother's vicious streak, too. She confronted him with all this made up crap. He was flabbergasted, and then he was devastated. He tried to convince Mariella she'd been fed a load of garbage, but she believed her mother. When he confronted Sharon about the whole situation that night, it all blew up."

Ava stopped and gathered her thoughts.

"She filed for divorce, threw Brian out of the house, then she and Mariella filed that fake complaint. That got Brian suspended from school, then charged with child abuse and the papers got hold of it..." her words trailed off. "Mariella's testimony made sure Brian was going to be convicted. When he heard it and saw the jury's reaction, he went home and blew his brains out."

"I am so sorry."

"Gina saw through a lot of it, even though she was only fifteen. She kept trying to tell the officials that Mariella was lying but they wrote her off, didn't take her seriously at all. After Brian killed himself, Sharon turned on that kid and absolutely ruined her life. Sharon told Gina she was wrong, a loser like her dad. Made the kid question every memory she ever had from her childhood. Gina would call me and tell me what was going on. She hung on to how she knew her Daddy wasn't that kind of guy and her mother crucified her for it."

"When did Gina come back to Fawcettville?"

"As soon as she turned eighteen, she left. I don't know why she went back to where Mom and Dad lived, but she did. Maybe she was trying to find some old family connections back in the New Tivoli neighborhood or something. I don't know. She already had a drug and alcohol problem, poor kid. It was her only way to escape her mother."

"I used to be a cop, and I arrested Gina a couple times. I can tell you she was homeless for a while."

"Oh God, no."

"She often prostituted herself to pay for her drugs or alcohol and was involved with a couple abusive men."

Ava was silent.

"I'm so sorry to tell you all this. So why did you leave Ohio?"

"The trial and Brian's suicide just ruined everything. Mom couldn't go anywhere without people whispering and pointing. Dad was heartbroken. He died within a couple months of Brian's suicide. It was the same for my family. Sam had an opportunity to transfer to San Francisco, so we packed up all our stuff and Mom and moved. We've been here ever since—the only time we came back was to bury Mom next to Dad in Pittsburgh. Nobody knows the Cantolini name out here."

"Do you have any contact at all with Sharon or Mariella?"

"Are you kidding? I wrote that bitch and her idiot daughter off long ago."

"I have to tell you, I talked to Sharon a couple hours ago."

"I'm sorry for you."

"No, actually, she sounded very timid, very unassuming."

"Yeah, well, that's part of the game she plays: sweet little long-suffering Sharon."

"She said she was in a wheelchair now and couldn't make it to Gina's funeral because she can't drive. Said she couldn't find anyone to bring her."

"She could tell me the sun comes up in the east and I wouldn't believe her. I not only wouldn't believe her, I'd call her doctor to verify the diagnosis and then find out where she bought the wheelchair and ask to see the receipt. That bitch is lying through her teeth."

I sighed. So Gina wasn't a victim of her father—both she and Daddy were the victim of a real Mommie Dearest. I remembered Gina's sad eyes in the back seat of my cruiser and understood. My victim tried to stand up for what is right and got beaten down for it. What kind of person did that to her own daughter?

"A couple years ago, I got a wedding invitation from Mariella. She was marrying some guy back there, but I don't remember the name. I threw the whole thing out."

"If I have anymore questions, can I call you back?"

"Sure. I want somebody to give that bitch everything she's got coming."

Chapter 13

I hung up the phone and leaned back in my chair. The morning was productive, but I sure didn't like what I found. And, sad as it was, it had nothing to do with who killed Gina—just the very painful story about family dynamics.

I hooked my fingers together behind my head, thinking back to my childhood. My parents were not so different than other New Tivoli families: they were loud in their every day conversations, whether it was in love or in anger. The arguments between my brothers and sisters were loud, too, but we never would have done what Sharon allegedly did to Brian Cantolini—or what Brian might have done to Mariella.

We Fitzhughs were fiercely loyal, from what the outside world could see, and would beat anybody bloody who challenged any one of us. But if you fucked up you got yours behind the oaken door of that white clapboard house in New Tivoli. More than once, my older brothers—Aidan, Jr., Randy and Mateo—came to my aid when I was a young and scrawny Nick the Mick, then beat my ass if they found out I'd instigated it. They saw less action in high school when I, too, developed Aiden Fitzhugh's broad shoulders and muscular, but bowed legs and no one dared approach me with any name that even hinted at an Irish or Italian slur.

I never knew what childhood sexual abuse was until I became a security policeman—SP in Air Force parlance—in Texas. I saw more of it as part of the FPD. It always generated a bottomless rage in me that dissipated as the perp's face got pounded into ground beef somewhere between my boxing gloves and the seventy-pound red Everlast bag in the corner of the YMCA gym.

But why concoct something so destructive and so violent and stuff it into a child's head? What kind of a mother would do that? Even if that child was an adult and more than a little gullible, as Ava intimated about Mariella, it was wrong.

Maybe Mariella was stupid and could be led by the nose at times, but we never know what really happens behind closed doors or in the dark of night. Maybe Ava supported her brother because she, too, couldn't believe what was being said in court. Maybe Brian really did commit these acts. The world only finds out when it somehow spills out into the street and we cops get to be the ones to clean it up.

Violation is violation and nobody willingly makes that shit up, right? What do I know? I still hadn't found out who—beside Michael Atwater—could have killed Gina Cantolini and that was what I was being paid to do.

Maybe my first impression of Atwater was right. Maybe he did do it. Michael Atwater had spent his life making anything but good choices. The argument could be made that his drug use and the violence between Gina and him had escalated to the point where he finally snapped. In his last bad decision, angry that Gina wanted a DNA test on her boys, as she was simultaneously demanding child support for them, he put his hands around her neck one last time and choked her unconscious and shot her with his own gun.

If that was so, why send someone like Jorge Rivera to scare me off this case? That's the other part I didn't get. Someone wanted Atwater railroaded for killing Gina. But who? And why?

Where was she killed? I hadn't found a killer, and I hadn't found a primary crime scene. Police believed they had the killer, but nothing was ever said about where he did it. If they had, that information should have been provided to Ambrosi. Maybe they didn't know either.

I sat back up. I had to put all this on the back burner for now. I had a little less than an hour to get ready for the benefit.

*****

Holding my first free drink of the evening, a watered down Jack and Coke, I wandered along the outer edges of Memorial Hall lobby, down by a table filled with items for a silent auction. The old antique benches that normally held the sedate bottoms of symphony attendees had been cleared away and replaced with large round tables. They were covered with white tablecloths, set with caterer's china and crowned with music themed centerpieces.

The evening's schedule had always been the same: provide as much free liquor through the cocktail hour and dinner to get folks to bid on items that ranged from Cleveland Browns tickets and gift baskets to golf trips, vacation condo rentals and symphony tickets. Just before the crowd moved into the main performance hall for the symphony's performance, the big donors would be recognized, and after the symphony played, the dancing would begin and the free drinks would end.

Tonight's performance featured some of the world's best-known cello concertos, with Gracie as the featured performer.

I watched as the guests wandered in: professors from the college, local politicians, and Fawcettville business leaders. They all stopped at the bar for their complimentary adult beverage and searched the round tables for their assigned seats before mingling with other attendees.

Before long, Dennis Lance and his staff entered, all of them wearing their 'Lance for Judge' tee shirts underneath their tuxedo jackets. Alicia Linnerman, filling out her tuxedo quite well, waved from across the room, and made a beeline toward me.

"Fitz! How are you?" She hugged me briefly.

I lifted my plastic cup. "Getting there."

"How's the Atwater case going?" She took a sip of her wine. Her cornflower blue eyes bored right through me, her round breasts pushing the limits of Dennis Lance's campaign shirt.

"Counselor, I can't tell you that. That's between my client and me. Heard anything from Officer Elliott?"

She shook her head. "No. There's a no-contact order in place. I have heard that Reno was terminated from the FPD, though."

"Before his case comes to court?"

Alicia smiled. "He's taking a guilty plea. Apparently your visit to the jail made him think it's best to own up to the assault charges rather than come back here to folks whispering about being involved in a murder."

I nodded. "Hopefully, he'll never be involved in law enforcement again."

"Yes. The chatter is whether or not he ever assaulted any other females."

"From what I heard he repeatedly asked my victim for sex and threatened her with arrest if she didn't come through."

"I thought we weren't talking about your case."

"Call it a small slip of the tongue. I can trust that you will see that information gets where it needs to go?" I looked over her head to see who else had wandered in. Alicia's boss was working the crowd as only a candidate could, pressing the flesh and handing out campaign literature. I wondered briefly if I should ask him about who paid for Gina Cantolini's funeral but thought the better of it.

"Of course."

From the corner of my eye, I caught Chief Monroe entering the lobby, along with his wayward spouse. She was dressed in a clingy black number that barely covered her ass and exposed more than a little cleavage. Maris saw I was looking her way and waved. The chief saw me, too, and jerked her close to keep her attention, nearly making her stumble.

Great. Just what I need—to be in the middle of whatever marital drama the Monroe's have going.

Alicia watched the exchange between them and snickered. "I've been doing a little research into you Fitz. I understand the Chief doesn't think a whole lot of you."

"It was seven years ago. People need to let that shit go."

Alicia leaned up against the wall next to me and sipped her drink. "Yeah, they do. But that's not how small towns work. You ought to know that."

"After that mess with Maris Monroe, I married my wife Gracie and we were very happy for a long time."

"Where is the esteemed Dr. Grace Darcy?"

"I haven't seen her yet."

"She doesn't know you're coming, does she?"

I was silent. Alicia didn't look me in the eye, but patted my arm sympathetically, not like the aggressive female I'd met just a few days before at her apartment.

"I thought so," she said. "Just by the way you said it the other day in my apartment."

"Yeah. Gracie wants me to sign the divorce papers like right now, but I just can't. I think she's dating someone —or wants to. She wants to get on with her life. I can't blame her."

"Neither can I," Alicia said, scanning the attendees as they walked through the door. "But sometimes it's just hard to let go of someone. Sometimes you just have to, whether you want to or not."

I leaned my head back against the old plaster wall and sighed.

"I can't. Not just yet."

"Well, come on then, Fitz. Neither one of us has dates, so let's at least pal around for the evening. No expectations, just for the laughs, just for the night." Alicia tugged on my sleeve. "Let's go say hello to all the muckety-mucks."

Turns out, Alicia was pretty good at glad-handing, just like her boss. We moved from table to table as the guests came in, smiling and making small talk. She only responded to campaign questions if directly asked, sending most folks over to the table where Lance was holding court, no doubt enjoying the fruits of yesterday's news story announcing his candidacy.

Slowly, the members of the symphony began to arrive and mingle with the guests. The crowd nearly doubled as the musicians entered, seemingly through the walls and, like fairies, lighting softly on the arms of last year's big donors, to weave their magic.

Then I saw her, entering the lobby from the performance hall. She wore a long black sequined dress, her long arms wrapped in an off white shawl that floated like ephemera behind her. She held a small black satin clutch close to her flat, toned stomach. Her hair was pinned up in a bun, as it always was for a performance, and she walked like a queen entering her kingdom.

In many ways, she was. That was one thing Gracie always liked about this event—she could talk to anybody about the symphony and her love of music. More often than not, she could coax someone up to the next rung on the donation ladder, getting funding for symphony trips into the public schools or scholarships for young musicians. She would, by the end of the evening, be circled by a throng of well-wishers and admirers, her throaty laugh bringing more to the fold and more money to the symphony's coffers.

I scanned the arched entrance behind her. Nobody followed her. She was alone. Maybe my fears about that pussy Van Hoven were unfounded.

"Excuse me," I whispered in Alicia's ear. "I'll be right back."

I caught up to my wife along the silent auction table.

"Hey, baby," I whispered, taking her arm.

Gracie jerked away.

"Goddammit Niccolo," she hissed. "What are you doing here?"

"Supporting the symphony, of course," I smiled. "And checking on my favorite cellist."

"I don't need checking on."

"Has anyone told you that you look wonderful tonight?"

"Has anyone told you you're a jerk?" She turned her attention back to the clipboards describing each silent auction item, writing down her bids and her office phone number.

"Baby, what you saw wasn't what it looked like. Judith Demyan was drunk. I'd just sent her proof that her husband was slipping it to that student on the side. She showed up at my office intoxicated and we weren't doing what it looked like. I wouldn't do that to you—I *love* you, Gracie. I was trying to push her off my lap when you came in."

"The fact that you let her get *onto* your lap is what pisses me off, Niccolo. If you weren't screwing her, she was giving you one hell of a lap dance and you were sure as hell enjoying it." Gracie moved down the display of auction items, stopping at a Cavaliers' gift basket, with an autographed LeBron James jersey, a couple tickets and a coffee mug.

I followed like the begging dog I was.

"Please, Gracie. That's not true. You gotta believe me."

She didn't answer. Another couple stepped up beside her to look at the gift basket. She grabbed my arm and pushed me toward other auction items farther down the table.

"Gracie, talk to me."

"I just want you to sign those divorce papers and get this whole mess over with."

"Give me just one more chance. We can make this work, honey. I know we can."

She stopped and sighed. "Don't you get it? I don't *want* to make it work. I want out. This might be my last quarter at the music department. My contract is up and I've been asked to interview at Berklee College of Music in Boston in June."

"You're leaving?" My heart hung in my chest.

"I might be. The college wants me to stay, but I'd be more than stupid to turn down Berklee if they offered it to me. That's the professional opportunity of a lifetime!"

"But you have a reason to stay here!"

"Do I?"

"Gracie, for God's sake, yes you do. Give me a chance. Give me one chance to make it up to you. If I can't make you see that all that stuff is behind me and all I want is you, then I'll sign the papers. You'll be free to go to Boston or wherever you want. I won't stand in your way."

She stopped looking over the silent auction items and turned to face me.

"Deal." She held out her hand. I shook it, and lifted it to my lips for a kiss. She jerked away. "Stop that. Not here!"

"So how is this going to work?"

"You tell me, Niccolo. Don't think you can just blow smoke up my skirt and think you can waltz back into my life, all charm and good times. It's going to take more than that. It's going to take some serious change on your part."

"I'll do whatever you want me to."

"That's not the point, Niccolo. The point is you have to convince me to stay. You have to convince me that won't ever happen again."

Gracie looked across the room and my gaze followed hers. Alicia Linnerman and Peter Van Hoven were approaching from opposite corners of the lobby. Alicia grinned at me and lifted her glass of wine in greeting; Dennis Lance was right behind her. Van Hoven was honing in on Gracie like a tuxedo-clad hunting dog going in for the kill. I wanted to lay my arm protectively around her waist, but knew she'd have no qualms about slugging me if I did.

Alicia approached first.

"Fitz, I thought I'd bring our esteemed judicial candidate over to say hello," she said, gesturing at her boss with her wine glass.

"Good to see you, Mr. Fitzhugh, as always." Lance reached out to shake my hand. "This time under better circumstances. That funeral the other day was something, wasn't it? Sad, sad situation."

"Yes, yes, it was. Mr. Lance, this is my wife, Dr. Grace Darcy. She's principal cellist here with the symphony. Grace, this is Dennis Lance, our prosecuting attorney and this is Alicia Linnerman, one of the staff assistant prosecutors."

Grace shot me a look: *I'm your wife in name only.* "Pleased to meet you, Mr. Lance."

Lance bowed formally. "Likewise. Alicia tells me, Fitz, you're working for Michael Atwater's defense team."

"Yes." If you want to call a burned-out lawyer and a former cop a team, go ahead. "I don't want to see someone go down for a murder he didn't commit."

"You've certainly got an uphill battle there," Lance smiled. "Next Friday, the grand jury meets. I have to say our case is pretty rock solid. I think we'll get an indictment."

I smiled with a confidence I didn't feel. "We'll see."

Van Hoven entered our conversation circle; Gracie politely introduced him as the new conductor. We chatted about his background, his aspirations for the symphony; Dennis Lance discovered their mutual love of golf.

"Do you play golf, Dr. Darcy?" Van Hoven asked politely.

" No, I don't." Their eyes met and sparkled with mutual attraction.

"My wife is the women's fencing coach for the college," I said, stepping closer to her. I touched the small of her back with my hand; the toe of her black ballerina flat struck my ankle. I cringed and dropped my hand. *Touché.*

"Yes, I am," answered Gracie, not missing a beat. "I really fell in love with the artistry and the athleticism of it. That, and golf bores me."

A short gray-haired woman in a cocktail dress came over and touched Van Hoven on the sleeve. I couldn't remember her name, but for years she'd been president of the Women's Symphony Association, the group that organized the benefit.

"It's time to begin the pre-dinner auction," she said politely.

"Ah, so it is." Van Hoven offered Gracie his arm and the two of them walked toward the podium.

"She's beautiful," Alicia said as soon as they were out of earshot.

"Yes she is," Lance agreed. "You're a lucky man, Fitz."

I took a gulp of my Jack and Coke. It was lukewarm and tasted like piss. "Tell me about it."

Alicia's blue eyes caught mine. She understood my pain—I could see that. I could also see that Reno Elliot wouldn't be the last bad boy she'd fall for. If I'd met her a few years earlier, before the disaster with Maris and the happiness I'd let slide away with Gracie, she might have been added to my list of broken hearts. The old Niccolo Fitzhugh wouldn't have thought twice. The old Niccolo would have done her and dumped her. Not now.

Alicia and Lance wandered off to find their seats. My glass was sweaty, like the palms of my hands. I sat it down on the table and headed toward the men's room.

What could I do to convince Gracie our marriage could work? Flowers, candy—the usual wouldn't do. She'd said as much. But what else could I do? Dinner at the restaurant where I'd asked her to marry me? Maybe that would be a good place to show her we were making a symbolic start. Maybe—

Maris Monroe grabbed me by the arm as she came out of the ladies' room.

"Hey sexy," she cooed.

"Get the hell away from me." I peeled her fingers, one by one, from my tuxedo sleeve.

"You just don't know a good thing when you see it," she smiled.

"If you're such a damned good thing, why did your husband try to shoot me? If you're such a good thing, why aren't you sitting next to—?"

The ladies' bathroom door opened and I stopped to stare at the woman who was coming out the door. She was taller than Alicia, and twice as juicy. She was shorter than Gracie, yet—I cringed as I realized it—without Gracie's elegant toughness. Real rocks, real diamonds, not like the cheap crystal knockoffs Maris wore, hung from this woman's ears and a string of single diamonds rested on a chain in the soft hollow of her throat, shimmering like the silver cocktail dress she wore. Her blue-black hair curled around her shoulders and her black brows arched perfectly over her dark brown eyes, edged in thick, black eyelashes. Her makeup was impeccable and her olive-colored skin had the toned, slightly rosy look of someone whose only reason for living consisted of drinking in the adulation of others. She looked like the kind of woman who wouldn't even let you in the door until her clothing was impeccable and her makeup was perfect and didn't care how long she made you wait.

Nations went to war over this kind of woman, and crimes were gladly committed in her name; the man who won her knew he had a trophy. In bigger cities or older societies, a woman like this would be the queen consort or the president's wife; she wouldn't give the time of day to a small town cop. "OUT OF YOUR LEAGUE" flashed over her head in three kinds of neon.

There was something in her face that I'd seen before, though. Maybe it was the curve of her nose, the arch of her sardonic smile, as she passed Maris and me on her way back into the benefit.

"So, you want to meet later for drinks?" Maris walked her fingers up my arm.

I pushed Maris's hand away and stared as the woman slipped through the arched lobby opening.

"Shut up. Get your sorry ass back to where you belong."

This dark-haired beauty walking away from me never knew anything but white-glove care and adoration from the moment she woke in the morning until she closed her eyes at night.

Or had she?

Take away the makeup, the fancy clothes and the hair, and she wasn't much different than a lot of folks in Fawcettville. Her Mediterranean looks made me think she was somehow tied to New Tivoli; one bad choice in her life could have changed her life's trajectory immensely, sending her to a job at the grocery store like Susan Atwater, rather than a life spent on a pedestal. And she didn't have to be the one who made the choice—it could have been made for her in the closing potteries and steel mills over the painful economic tides this town suffered over the years.

Put a scarf around the neck, add the damage of an abusive boyfriend plus the hard mileage of addiction then top it off with some cheap dollar-store clothing—I knew suddenly where I'd seen that face.

It was in Gina Cantolini's casket.

Chapter 14

I followed the silver dress back into the lobby and, on a hunch, called out to her.

"Mariella! Mariella Cantolini!"

She didn't respond.

I called her name again and tapped her on her shoulder.

She stopped and turned around this time, her dark eyes swallowing me whole. Could this be the manipulative little shit whose lies led to her father's suicide? Who got talked into false memories of sexual abuse and testified to them in court? This creature seemed to be too smart and too savvy to be manipulated by anyone.

"Excuse me? Do I know you?" Her voice was warm caramel and sex stirred together, but there was no sign she'd recognized the name.

"Mariella—I thought that was you! It's me, Nick Fitzhugh. I went to school with your aunt and your dad. I haven't seen you since you were this high." Amazing how easily I lied to get what I wanted. Maybe Gracie was right. It would take a lot more to convince her I'd changed.

"I'm sorry. I think you have me confused with someone else."

"I could have sworn Ava Cantolini was your aunt and Brian Cantolini was your dad. They lived just a couple block from my folks in New Tivoli."

"No, I'm so sorry. My name is Rachel Lance. My husband is the prosecutor, Dennis Lance."

Of course — lucky bastard.

"That's where I've seen you then," I backpedaled. "I work very closely with the courts. I must have seen you at his office. My apologies."

The warm caramel voice cooled considerably. "Yes. Excuse me, please."

I watched as she sauntered over to her husband and his staff. Lance stood as Rachel approached and pulled back a chair for her to sit. She descended gracefully into the chair; Lance sat down beside her and draped his arm around her shoulder. She snuggled under his arm and looked back at me with a smirk. *I am used to being approached by men like you,* she seemed to say, *and you can't afford me.*

So I was wrong.

This case was getting to me. Rachel Lance may have looked like a lot of the folks from my old neighborhood, but from her reaction she clearly wasn't a Cantolini.

I found an empty seat at the back of the room and accepted the salad, along with a cup of weak coffee, from a server. I watched Gracie as she sat at the head table, talking with Van Hoven. There was an empty chair next to her. I'd sat there in years past; no doubt the organizers saw my name on the list of attendees and assumed I'd be there again. *Next year I will be.* After the meal of rubber chicken, asparagus and some sort of potato, Gracie was back up at the podium, introducing one of the local auctioneers, who led the charge to get the most money from those well-lubricated pockets. The crowd grew louder as the after-dinner liquor began to flow and Gracie worked the crowd, encouraging attendees to wave their bidder numbers and call out their ever-increasing offers.

When she wasn't working the crowd, she was beaming at any attention Van Hoven paid her. I watched Van Hoven whisper something in her ear; Gracie threw back her head and laughed, shooting him an intimate, knowing look. I'd been the recipient of that look, too, once upon a time.

That's it. I can't watch anymore of this. I slipped out before the auction ended and walked back to my Expedition. The sun was setting in the west and the smell of a spring evening filled the air.

What could I do to convince her to come back to me, to make her stay here in Fawcettville rather than packing up and leaving for Boston? God knows Berklee College of Music will hire her in a heartbeat.

Footsteps echoed through the parking lot as I pulled my keys from my pocket. The hairs on the back of my head stood on edge: I knelt as if to tie my shoe, slipping my fingers around the grip of the Kahr P9 in my ankle holster. I'd been cold cocked once this week and it wasn't going to happen again.

From my vantage point, I saw scrawny legs running between the rows of cars, heard teenage laughter and profanity, followed by the rasp of skateboard wheels along the pavement. Relieved, I exhaled and stood up.

A hairy arm hooked around my throat and squeezed, cutting off my oxygen. Colors popped in my field of vision as I struggled to free myself.

"I told you to leave this case alone," a familiar raspy voice hissed in my ear. I felt a cold blade under my left ear.

" That you, Rivera, or the ghost of pussies past?"

Clutching his arm, I spun around and body-slammed him into the Expedition's rear door, jamming my elbow into his soft gut. He groaned and let go of me, sinking to the ground. I kicked the knife under the Expedition and pulled Rivera back up by his collar.

"Fuck you, Fitzhugh," he spat.

Rivera's nose met my fist and blood spurted down his shirt. I let him slide down to the ground again and kicked him in the ribs. Rivera curled up on his side, holding his face.

" You're welcome," I said, shaking the pain from my knuckles. "I thought somebody plugged you in the alley."

Rivera tried to get to his feet. I kicked him again and he sank back to the pavement.

"I said, didn't somebody shoot you in the alley?" I leaned over him, speaking slowly and loudly, enunciating my words.

"No," Rivera groaned. "I got him. He was checking to make sure I did what I was paid to do."

"And you didn't, did you?" I stepped back and let Rivera stand up.

Rivera roared in rage and came at me again. With a short sideways kick, I knocked him off balance and he fell again, face first, into the pavement.

"Whoever you're working for needs to send in the first team. You've had two chances to push me off this case and failed. Now get the fuck out of here and tell your handlers to send a real man to do the job next time."

Maybe I shouldn't have let him go. Maybe I should have beat the shit out of him right there, but hell, the tux was rented and I just wanted to get home. I adjusted my bow tie in the window as Rivera stood.

"You don't know who you're messing with," Rivera stood, wiping his bloody nose on his sleeve.

" I know I'm messing with somebody who wants to see an innocent man go to prison for a murder he didn't commit," I said as I turned to face him. "I know you have connections to Reno Elliot, who threatened my victim. What else do I need to know?"

"It's more than that," Rivera said.

"What do you mean?"

Rivera looked around. His shoulders sank. I sensed he wanted to talk. I pulled a handkerchief from my jacket and handed it to him.

"Clean yourself up and meet me at Puccini's."

"I'm not sure exactly where that is."

"Don't bullshit me. I know you've met Reno Elliot there."

Rivera stared at his feet. "OK."

"Twenty minutes, tops."

*****

I was sitting in one of the red booths in the center of Puccini's window when my waitress sat a cannoli and a cup of espresso in front of me. I was halfway through both when Rivera, both eyes turning blue and purple from my blow to his nose, slid into the booth seat across from me. He'd taken the time to change his shirt—and maybe tell his handlers.

I signaled to the waitress, ordering the same thing for him.

She brought his order, and I waited for him to take a bite of his cannoli before I spoke.

"So what's the deal behind all this? Who wants to see Michael Atwater convicted and why?"

"There's more here than you think. Do we have to sit here where the whole world can see us?"

"What are you afraid of?"

"Your victim knew something, something people in power didn't want anyone else to know," Rivera began, looking nervously out the window. "That's why she was killed."

"OK. Like what?" Gina had a lot of pain in her life, but as for knowing something that mattered enough for someone in power to kill her? I had my doubts.

"I don't know. I just know that they figured it would be easy to pin the murder on the one boyfriend. They knew about the DNA testing because that had been court ordered. They knew about the other boyfriend, too—"

"Jacob Poole?"

Before Rivera could answer, I caught a glimpse of a vehicle slowing in the street outside. The window on the passenger side came down, and the streetlight caught the glint of a silver handgun.

"Look out!" I yelled.

Bullets shattered the glass as the waitress screamed and I dove beneath the table, glass shards flying. Pulling my Kahr from my ankle holster, I peeked over the edge of the broken window to catch a few numbers on the license plate. Tires squealed as the vehicle, a boxy, nondescript sedan, pulled off down the street.

"Everybody OK?" I crawled out from beneath the table, gun in hand. The waitress, a college kid, came up from behind the counter, her hands shaking and black mascara coursing down her cheeks with her tears. The antique brass espresso machine behind her was pocked with bullet holes and the mirror behind it was shattered. Rivera was silent. The waitress screamed again and I saw why: half of his face was gone, and his brains were splattered against the back of the red booth.

So he meant what he said. Somebody seriously wanted me off this case.

The waitress dialed 911, screaming the details of what happened to the dispatcher. I called Detective Joe Barnes on my cell and he arrived as quickly as the police. After the crime-scene technician swabbed my hands for gunshot residue, he pulled me off to the side to talk to me while the coroner and her staff looked over what was left of Rivera. Another detective was interviewing the waitress.

"So what happened, Fitz?"

"You can't tell?"

"Don't be a smartass. I just want to know how you ended up in the middle of a murder."

"The victim and I met in the Memorial Hall parking lot—I was leaving the symphony benefit. We had a little unpleasantness between us, frankly, and I was forced to defend myself. The coroner might ask you about that, he might not. After seeing my point of view, Rivera had some information he wanted to tell me. I said we should meet here at Puccini's and discuss it over coffee. We were each having a cannoli and espresso when this car drove by really slowly. I saw a gun come out the passenger-side window and the next thing I know, I'm under the table, covered in broken glass."

"What did Rivera want to talk to you about?"

"The Cantolini case, but that's all I know."

"Don't bullshit me, Fitz. I remember you calling and asking me if I knew anybody by that name."

"That was after I found he was tailing me. I finally caught him in the alley by Lupe's, but I never did learn anything about him."

"You sure those bullets weren't meant for you?"

"Why would they be?"

"I know somebody who's still got a real grudge over something that happened a while back."

"Not the chief. You're kidding me, right?"

Barnes just arched an eyebrow.

"I can't believe that, Joe. C'mon."

Barnes shrugged. "He's known to carry a grudge."

"Trust me, Maris Monroe can take her delights elsewhere. I'm not interested."

"I don't know if he exactly believes that." If it had been fifty years ago and life was black and white, Barnes would have been in a trench coat, pushing his pork pie hat up off his forehead with his thumb as he talked. Tonight, he was in khaki pants and a blue FPD polo shirt, his badge and his service revolver anchored on his belt, but the effect was the same.

We watched silently as Rivera, now encased in a black vinyl body bag, rolled by on a gurney.

"It's been a long time since we've had two murder cases in a week in this town," Barnes continued. "The world is going to hell in a hand basket if you ask me. If you find anything out, give me a call. You know where to find me."

He followed the gurney out the door. There wasn't much more for me to do either; I left soon after.

Back at my office, I flopped into my desk chair and pulled the bourbon, along with a cup, out of the bottom drawer. I poured two fingers worth and sighed.

If what Rivera said was correct, if Gina Cantolini had information that disturbed the powers that be, what could it be? Was it worth killing her over?

And what if Barnes was right? What if that bullet was meant for me and not Rivera? I have no doubt the chief saw Maris hanging all over me near the restrooms—and if it wasn't him, one of his minions told him about it. That broad had nearly been the death of me once and maybe tonight, she was again.

I gulped down the bourbon, stepped into the office bathroom and out of my tux. The jacket was smeared with cannoli filling and dirt from Puccini's floor. It smelled like espresso. The pants weren't much better. I picked a couple of pieces of glass out of one of the jacket's shoulders. I'd be paying a cleaning fee on this sucker when I dropped it off Monday. I stepped into some sweatpants and an old FPD

T-shirt and brushed my teeth, leaving the Kahr hanging in the holster on the bathroom door. Back in the waiting room, I pulled my pillows and blanket from behind the couch; just like every other night, I lay my Glock next to my cell phone on the coffee table and switched out the lights.

*****

The window in my office door shattered and I shot up from the couch, grabbing my Glock. Flames flashed along the floor and onto the cheap rug beneath my feet as the smell of gasoline filled the air. Smoke seared my lungs as I tried to beat the flames down with the blanket, trying to make my way to the door. The fire alarm in the hallway began to howl and flash, adding to the confusion.

Behind me, in my office, I heard a noise on the fire escape outside my office window. The glass there shattered and I saw the flash of another Molotov cocktail striking my office floor, the flame spreading up the thin curtains and across the ceiling.

I had to get in there before it caught fire. Stuffing my Glock in my waistband, and throwing the blanket over my head, I charged into the office. The Atwater case file—Ava Jones' and Sharon Hansen's phone numbers, my laptop with the web sites about Brian Cantolini's sex abuse trial, the police reports Ambrosi gave me about the murder —all lay across my desk. *No! I can't lose those!*

The dry wood of my chair ignited, flames licking dangerously close to the desk. I grabbed what I could—the outer housing on my laptop was beginning to blacken with smoke, but maybe the hard drive would survive.

I turned back toward the waiting room; a wall of flame greeted me, blocking my exit out that door. Smoke was filling the office—and my lungs. Sparks were landing on the blanket, igniting circles of flames. Drawing a rasping breath, I dropped the blanket and swiveled back toward my office. The curtains hung in burning strips around the window. I clutched the laptop close to my chest and pushed my way out the window and on to the fire escape.

The first fire truck pulled up to the curb as I collapsed on the sidewalk, the laptop clattering beside me. A firefighter jumped from the truck and ran to me.

"Somebody threw two Molotov cocktails into my office," I gasped.

"Is there anyone else in the building?" he asked, before covering my mouth with an oxygen mask.

I shook my head and drew more oxygen into my seared lungs. As I watched the fire crews battle the blaze, I couldn't help but think that Lt. Barnes was right.

The bullets that hit Rivera —and now, the Molotov cocktails—were meant for me.

Chapter 15

Barnes was at the hospital by the time my ambulance arrived at the ER.

"What did I tell you, Fitz?" he asked as they unloaded me from the back of the truck. "Somebody's after your ass and they're serious about it."

I shrugged from behind my oxygen mask, clutching my laptop to my chest. There was too much on it to turn it over to the cops—or the prosecutor's office—provided it had survived the fire.

Barnes followed my gurney into the ER, flashing his badge at the medical staff there.

Between gulps of oxygen and the attention of the medical staff to my burned face, arms and feet, I told Barnes what happened. Since I was asleep when the first Molotov hit, I had no description of any suspects. He nodded continuously as he took notes.

"That pretty much squares with what the fire department found: two incendiary devices, most likely glass bottles filled with gasoline and rags. One came through the front door; the other came through the window," he said, shoving his notebook into his back pocket. "The question is why? What are you working on, Fitz? I mean, besides the Cantolini case? I can't imagine any wayward husbands being this pissed at being caught. Is it on that laptop? You're hanging on to it pretty damned tightly."

"Yeah. Most of my office files are on there, including the Atwater case. I grabbed it before I went through the window."

Barnes smirked. "Atwater's an open-and shut-case. I'm sure what you've dug up squares with what we found at his arrest. What's the phrase—'billable hours'? If you don't find anything else, you'll get a pile of cash from that."

I shrugged. "If I found something else, which I haven't, we'd turn it over to you." That much was true. But why was someone trying so hard to keep me from doing that? Clearly there was something someone wanted to hide.

"Well, Ambrosi's got to make it look like he's at least trying to get the kid off, I suppose. I've never known a more half-assed lawyer in my whole life." Barnes shook his head. "Between you and me and these lovely ladies—" Barnes nodded at the nurses around me. "I think you know who's behind this."

I started to answer, but began to cough again. Go ahead and think the chief still wants my ass. This is more than a cuckolded husband going for the most obvious target.

The curtain surrounding my bed whipped open. It was Gracie, still in her black sequined gown and clutching her white shawl and purse, her eyes wide with concern.

"Niccolo! What happened? Are you OK?" She ran to my bedside, clasping my one free hand.

I coughed as I nodded. "I'm going to be OK."

"Listen, it looks like I've got everything I need here," Barnes said. "I'll leave you two alone. Fitz, I'll call you if I need anything else. That includes that laptop." The nurses also stepped out.

As soon as we were alone, Gracie dropped her shawl and clutch on the bed and clasped my burned cheeks to kiss my forehead.

I gasped in pain.

"Oh baby, I'm sorry!" She dropped her hands, but her soft lips kept contact with my skin.

"How did you know I was here?" I tried to speak through the mask, but started coughing again. She sat up and began to run her long fingers through my smoky hair.

"When the alarm went off, the security company called the guy who owns the jewelry store downstairs—Mr. Grundy. He called the house to tell you about the fire," she said. Her tone became soft, contrite. "I didn't tell him you'd been sleeping there."

I sank back into the pillows and sighed. "I don't know where I'm going to go, Gracie. I don't know if I have anything left. All my files, all my papers—they're probably gone. Anything I have left is on this laptop."

Gracie laid her forehead on my shoulder, tears wetting the shoulder of my hospital gown. I caressed her soft dark hair, drinking in her perfume. *Thank you, oh God, thank you,* I thought, closing my eyes.

"I was so upset when I heard the building was on fire," she whispered into my shoulder. "I went right over there. I got there just after they put you in the ambulance, so I came right over here."

"It's OK. So you were already back at home? What about you and Van Hoven? Did your performance go OK?"

She raised her head and looked me in the eye, smiling. "Van Hoven is a dog—and yes, I have to say my performance tonight was stellar. I think we raised a lot of money."

"Glad it went well —and you saw through him. What happened with you two?"

She sat up and kissed me again, soft and lingering.

"None of your business."

"You're right. I have no right to pry into your personal life. It's none of my business." *Another sign she was moving on.*

"We'll talk about that later. What I do want is for you to come home, Niccolo."

"Are you saying there's hope for us, Gracie?" I couldn't believe what she was saying.

"This doesn't mean you're home free or that I've forgiven you. We still have a long way to go. But come home."

A nurse, her stethoscope hanging from her neck, came back to my bedside.

"Oh, he won't be coming home tonight. We're going to keep him overnight, to make sure he gets all the stuff out of his lungs. We also need to run some more tests and those can't be done until tomorrow, maybe Monday."

I handed the laptop to Gracie. Another paroxysm of coughing overtook me. "Take this with you. I couldn't keep it here anyway. Don't let anyone see it or take it," I managed to gasp.

"I will."

"And ma'am?" The nurse handed her a plastic bag of my clothing. "Please take this home as well. Hospital policy prohibits firearms in patient rooms."

Chapter 16

By Sunday afternoon, I was out of the hospital. Gracie drove me back to the office before heading home and we stood together on the sidewalk, just in time to watch seven years of my burned up life get chucked out the window of my office and into a Dumpster.

Thankfully, the damage was limited to my office and the upstairs hallway—nothing in Grundy's jewelry store or the two offices on either side of mine. The excellent work of firefighters, though, wouldn't convince Grundy to let me be his tenant ever again.

Me, I didn't look much better than what remained of my office. I had burn cream on my cheeks to stop the pain and my bandaged legs stuck out from beneath the cut-off shorts Gracie brought me to wear home from the hospital. She brought a pair of flip-flops to cover my bandaged feet.

Barnes was at the scene, working with the fire investigators. He leaned out the window and waved.

"Fitz, I found something you're probably looking for," he called. His big, flat feet clattered down the stairs to the street. At the doorway, he tossed my cellphone to me.

"Hey, asshole, my fucking hands are burned. I can't —*ouch!"* I managed to grab my iPhone with my bandaged paws before it hit the ground. I handed it to Gracie. Barnes smirked as I shook the pain away.

"I don't know how it happened, but that sumbitch survived without burning. Damnedest thing," he said. "Found it under a file cabinet."

"Does it work?" Gracie pushed the power button.

"Oh yes. I already checked it —and all the calls you've made in the last few days," Barnes grinned. "Don't worry, you're in the clear. We don't think you had anything to do with this—or Rivera's killing."

He stepped out of the way as four firefighters, each holding the corner of a blue tarp, came down the office stairs. They spread the tarp on the sidewalk and waved me over so I could see if there was anything worth saving.

Gracie and I slipped inside the ring of crime-scene tape and crouched next to the pile. I found the cuff links I'd worn Saturday night and what was left of the black cummerbund, along with my coffee mug. The plastic exterior of the coffeemaker was melted, exposing the metal innards, and the pot was broken. My leather ankle holster still held my Kahr 9, but there wasn't much left of either. I couldn't recognize anything else, even what was left of our wedding portrait, which had sat on my desk.

"Niccolo, look what I found..." Gracie pulled at something beneath a stack of burned magazines. It was my KSU football hoodie—or what was left of it. Black soot coated what was left of one sleeve; flames had crept up the back and side, eating away the lettering across the back—and with its destruction, my youth.

I rocked back on my heels and hung my head, but didn't say anything.

"That hoodie was way past its prime," she said gently. "Let it go."

"Yeah, there's a lot of things I need to let go of," I said softly.

The fire crew brought down a filing cabinet; it was covered in ash, but intact. I stood and traced my initials in the black ash. Nearly everything in the office was gone. My Expedition had been parked at the sidewalk during the fire. The paint across the hood bubbled but that was the only damage. Thank God for that—I'd left my camera and video surveillance equipment in there.

"Looks like some of your files survived," Barnes said.

"Yeah," I said, opening and closing a drawer, just to see if it worked.

"Nothing in there has the name Atwater on it," Barnes said.

"No, those files were all spread out on my desk."

"They're gone then." Barnes grimaced. "All the evidence of who set your place on fire has burned up too."

The wounds on my legs began to throb. I slipped under the crime-scene tape and hobbled slowly back to Gracie's Volvo. I sat down in the passenger seat, motioning for Barnes to follow me.

"About what you were saying about the chief being behind this..." I began. "You weren't serious, were you?"

Barnes shrugged. "We have to look at everything. But I'm not going to be the asshole that claims the chief of police had a private dick's office firebombed, just because I can. We've got to have something that could lead us in that direction. That would require bringing in state investigators, since we aren't big enough to have an internal affairs department. Shit, that would end anybody's career—his if it's true and mine if it's not. I'm too damned close to getting my pension, Fitz."

"I haven't talked to Nathan Monroe since I retired from the FPD seven years ago. Every time Maris Monroe approaches me, I tell her to pound sand." *Monroe and I haven't spoken since he shoved a gun in my face and threatened to kill me, at any rate.*

"Yeah, and she's pounded just about everybody on the force." Barnes leaned one of his bony arms on the Volvo's roof. "I suppose you're right there. If he firebombed the home of every one of the guys she slept with, half this town would be leveled."

"Honestly, I don't think he's involved, Barnes. I don't know who it could be, though." He didn't need to know I thought it was someone connected with the Atwater case. But who?

"If we find something about the Chief that's credible to lead us down that path, we're obligated to follow it. You know that," Barnes said.

"I know. I just don't think you will."

Gracie joined us. The three of us watched as another load of debris—the burned-up couch and what was left of my desk—sailed through the window and into the Dumpster. Everything I worked for, even the best memories of my short-lived college career, were gone.

"Do you need anything more from Niccolo, Detective? I've got to get him home."

"No, I guess not. Just don't leave town."

I gestured toward my legs and feet with my bandaged hands. "Do I look like I could get very far?"

*****

I had Gracie take my equipment from the Expedition and put it in the Volvo. We found a clean tarp and had the firefighters lift the file cabinet into the Volvo as well.

I decided to leave the Expedition sitting in front of the burned-out office for now—no sense in parking my truck in front of her house and putting her in danger. *I'll call Ambrosi on Monday and see if I can work out of his office for a few weeks. I can leave the Expedition parked at his office after it's repaired.*

She slammed the Volvo's hatch closed and slid into the driver's seat. I reached over to put my hand on her leg. She patted my arm and then moved my hand back to my lap.

"I meant what I said Niccolo," she said gently. "I want you back home because you haven't got any place else to go—that doesn't mean we're back on track."

I let my head fall back against the back of my seat. "I can't convince you, can I?"

The Volvo slid into the traffic. Gracie didn't speak for a few blocks, until we were out of the downtown and closer to the polished neighborhood around the college where her house stood.

"When we started dating, a lot of people told me that I was getting in over my head. I knew you had a reputation with the ladies and frankly, weren't one to keep your pecker in your pants," she said. "I was warned by everyone—the cops you'd worked with, even your mother —not to marry you."

"I know."

"But I married you anyway. I've spent the last six years knowing what you've done and knowing those angry women who hire you want to sleep with you to pay their husbands back. I spent six years wondering if you crossed that line."

"I never did, Gracie, I never did."

We pulled up the driveway. She stopped the car. "When I saw Judy Demyan on your lap, all those warnings, all those little niggling voices in the back of my head—they came back."

" We had six good years, Gracie. You were the only one all through those six years and you still are the only one. Don't let this—us—go down the crapper."

I couldn't say anything else. Silently, we entered the house and Gracie led me to the guest room.

"There you go," she said. "I'm going to go ask the neighbor if he can help get that filing cabinet out of the back of the car."

I waited until I heard the front door slam before I looked around.

She'd moved what was left of my clothing into the closet and set the laptop up on the desk there. I'd be sleeping on an antique four-poster bed we'd found during a weekend antiquing safari into Amish country. I knew the mattress wasn't the best, but it had to be better than the last thirty days on the office couch.

The matching dresser had an antique doily on top, anchored by a pastel blue and white porcelain figurine of a woman playing a cello and a framed, autographed picture of Yo-Yo Ma. The top three drawers were empty. I opened the bottom drawer and found our wedding picture—the one Ma took of Gracie and me standing in front of a beaming judge—laying face down on a stack of blankets.

Clutching the photo, I sank down on the bed and sighed. My copy of the picture was destroyed in the fire.

Would my marriage go up in smoke, like that photo, or would it live, like this one? I sat the picture on the nightstand by my bed.

I had to come up with a way to convince her to stay.

*****

Soon after, the pain pills kicked in, sending me into a deep slumber. I awoke several hours later to the smell of Ma's marinara sauce. Rubbing my eyes as well as my bandages would allow, I followed the aroma downstairs and into the kitchen.

"There he is!" Ma threw her birdlike hands into the air and shuffled toward me in her orthopedic shoes.

"No hugs—don't touch the face," I said, leaning over to kiss her.

"So Gracie called me last night to tell me what happened. I wanted to come visit you in the hospital this morning, but they let you go before I could get there," Ma said, returning to the stove and taking a wooden spoon from Gracie. "Niccolo, you aren't a cop anymore. This business of yours, it's too dangerous and you're too old to be running around with a gun. Why don't you go back to school, get a business degree? I'm sure you could get a nice safe job where you sit behind a desk and don't get shot at."

Gracie covered her mouth with her hand to suppress a smile. The thought of me doing anything other than being a PI was as likely as me learning to speak Chinese.

"Ma, would Dad have ever done anything else other than be a cop?"

"Gracie, stir the penne for me, please. Niccolo, you don't know the times I asked him to quit the force. Every time your father went to work, I never knew if he would come home to me. Like that time Aidan nearly got his brains beat out, responding to a bar fight at Gino's Bar and Grill. It took him and three other officers to stop that fight."

"I don't remember that."

"Of course not! You weren't born yet! There I was, three children under five and pregnant with my fourth—that was you, Niccolo—and I'd just lost my father, who you were named for, and my Aidan, he's in the emergency room, his head looking like the sauce in that pot. Terrible. It was terrible, Gracie. My Aidan, God rest his soul, had headaches for days, I tell you, *days.*"

I shook my head. There were a few rough days in my dad's career, but like most small town cops, he may have pulled his weapon a couple times, but he never fired it. I wish I could have said the same thing. The meth and the heroin that infested the streets had changed the face of police work and police response in Fawcettville. I'd pulled my service revolver more than once—and the one time in twenty years I fired, I didn't miss. Most nights, it didn't bother me; some nights I sat up in bed covered in cold sweat, once again believing I was cornered with no way out.

"Anyway, I'm glad to see you are back home, Niccolo, back where you belong," she finished. I looked over at my wife, who made a locking motion at her lips. "Now Gracie, set the table and we'll have dinner. The salad is in the fridge."

Chunks of *salsiccia fresca*, the fresh sweet Italian sausage that Ma bought at the lone butcher shop at the edge of town, rested along with the marinara on the bed of penne pasta in a bowl at the center of the table. Gracie opened a bottle of wine and brought it to the table. Rather than pass the steaming bowl, we served ourselves. Seated between Gracie and me, Ma handed around a bowl of shredded Parmesan, followed by the salad.

It could have been any Sunday afternoon in New Tivoli during my childhood.

Back then, Dad sat at the head of the table as we enjoyed our lunch following Mass. We were rowdy and loud except for the few moments Ma shushed us so Dad could say the blessing. If he wasn't working, he got to sit in front of the new color TV set and watch the Steelers or the Pirates play, one or more of us kids lounging against and around him. Most Sundays, though, he shed his Sunday suit and, in his uniform pants and white T-shirt, ate his pasta, and drank copious amounts of black coffee instead of wine. After he ate, with his uniform shirt sharply ironed and his service revolver around his waist, he headed off for his twelve-hour shift.

After he retired, he could watch every game he wanted following Ma's enormous pasta meal. By then, his lap was filled with grandchildren; my brothers, none of them cops, could sit and watch with him. I was the one, this time, dashing in from my own Sunday shift and hanging my uniform shirt on the doorknob to enjoy Ma's pasta.

Now, Dad was gone, and each of my sisters and brothers had their own families with their own Sunday dinners. They took turns taking Ma home from Mass with them for their tables full of steaming pasta—we all did, Gracie and me included.

Today's meal was like one of those sweet Sundays all over again. Gracie thought that too—I could see it in her face. She loved those Sundays as much as I did—they certainly had to be more fun than anything she experienced in that cold Connecticut house of her parents. She often helped Ma clean up the kitchen, since Ma insisted on washing the dishes, no matter at whose house we ate, and we could all hear Gracie's deep throaty laugh all the way out into the living room. My sisters loved her, too. More than once, someone leaned over my shoulder to hand me another beer and whispered, "You got lucky with this one, Nick. You need to hang on to her."

When I began sleeping in my office, with no place to fix a meal, I begged off my slot in the rotation. Now here I was, back in the batting order and knew if I didn't hit it out of the park this time, I would once again be the irresponsible brother.

I lifted my glass of dago red with a bandaged hand. Gracie and Ma followed suit.

"A toast," I said. "To my favorite girls. I'm so very lucky to have you both. I hope you feel the same way. *Salud!*"

"*Salud!* Now shut up, Niccolo," Ma said. "Eat your pasta before it gets cold."

"Yeah, Niccolo," Gracie echoed, her eyes misting. "Shut up."

Chapter 17

The sun was midway through the morning sky when I began to pry my eyes open. I pulled the blankets up over my shoulder and savored, for the moment, the feel of the cool cotton sheets and the clean smell of the pillow beneath my head. *God, this is so much better than my office couch.* I rolled over and gasped, startled at the curving, feminine silhouette beneath the blanket beside me. Too much wine at dinner hadn't affected me so much that I forgot Gracie coming to bed with me, had it? Sweet Mary, Mother of God, I wouldn't do that.

I reached over with a bandaged paw to touch, to see if it were really Gracie.

Shit. The wad of pillows and blankets collapsed beneath my hand and disappointment seeped into my now-awake brain. I sighed and swung my legs over the side of the bed.

Enough dreaming. It was Monday, and I had things to do.

Wandering into the kitchen, I rubbed my fingers through my hair, planning my day. I needed to talk to Mike or Susan Atwater to see if Gina ever told them about her father's suicide and the twisted vengeance that led to her destructive lifestyle. It may not have anything to do with finding who really killed her, but you never know. I also needed to drop by Ambrosi's office to see if I could work there for a few weeks until I found a more permanent place to settle and get the Expedition into the shop to repair that bubbled paint.

On the kitchen table, there was a note and a set of car keys from Gracie beneath an empty coffee cup:

"Niccolo—here's the keys to the Volvo. One of the other Profs took me to work this morning so you could have the car, in case you needed it. There's coffee in the pot. Pick me up at 4:30—G."

I couldn't be too much in the dog house if she wanted me to pick up her up after work, could I? Mentally, I added "buy flowers" to my to-do list for the day.

I punched the 'on' button at the side of the coffeemaker and unrolled the morning edition of the *Fawcettville Times*. It wasn't a bad little paper— a lot of reporters, good and bad, got their start there before moving on, moving up or moving out of the business entirely.

While I was a cop, I had a couple hot weekends with the crime reporter, a Harley-riding woman named Bobbie, who had a way with words like no one I'd ever met. Before Bobbie rode off to the Pittsburgh *Post-Gazette* and out of my life, she called me dog—more specifically, a horny Rottweiler who'd hump anything from a Shih Zhu to a hole in a tree. I was also a pig whose lack of commitment spread deep down into my DNA. I couldn't manage anything more creative than to call her a fucking crazy, workaholic, badge bunny. The day she roared off on her motorcycle was a good day indeed.

This wasn't one of those good days: scrawled across the top of the *Times* was a sickening headline:

Weekend Violence Centers on Local PI

A local private investigator and former Fawcettville police officer is at the center of a murder and a firebombing, both of which occurred Saturday night.

Jorge Rivera, age and address unavailable, was shot and killed at Puccini's coffee shop, a long-time landmark in the New Tivoli neighborhood, during a meeting with private investigator Niccolo Fitzhugh, of Fitzhugh Investigations.

According to reports, Fitzhugh reported seeing a dark-colored, boxy sedan traveling slowly down in front of the coffee shop. The passenger-side window came down, a weapon was displayed and shots were fired into the coffee shop window, killing Rivera.

Further information about Rivera was not available at press time, although sources connected with the investigation suggested he might have been an undercover operative of some sort.

Later that same night Fitzhugh was apparently working late at his office when two suspects tossed what fire investigators believe to be Molotov cocktails through Fitzhugh's front office door and through the office window from the fire escape.

Damages to Puccini's coffee shop were estimated at approximately $10,000. Damages to Fitzhugh's office could total $50,000, according to building owner Orville Grundy.

Fitzhugh was not injured in the shooting, however, he did suffer first- and second-degree burns and smoke inhalation as a result of the fire. Fitzhugh was hospitalized in good condition and expected to be released Monday.

"We have no idea what kind of dangerous activity Mr. Fitzhugh is involved in, but clearly he's being targeted for something," said Chief Nathaniel Monroe.

Fitzhugh served twenty years with the Fawcettville police before retiring suddenly seven years ago to start his own private investigations firm, Monroe said.

His personnel file, provided by Monroe at the request of the *Times*, showed several citations for bravery and service. Performance reviews over the years were largely positive, however, Monroe said, "Fitzhugh's decisions in his personal life could sometimes interfere with his professional life."

This is the second murder in Fawcettville this month and the first arson committed in three years. Slightly more than a week ago...

I didn't need to read anymore. I knew as public employees, a cop's personnel record was open to anyone who asked—within reason, at least, in the state of Ohio. Information such as my address would be redacted for my own protection. At least it was supposed to be. Would Monroe let that information slip?

The only incorrect information was my release date from the hospital, but if things at the *Times* operated the same way they did while Bobbie was still there, the story was likely written before I was sent home. It's also possible the reporter tried to contact me and failed. I don't even remember seeing anyone resembling a reporter—any cop could spot one at any crime scene—at the fire or at Puccini's.

But why identify Rivera as an "undercover operative?" Was he an undercover cop or a confidential informant? Would Monroe throw one of his own, particularly one who just gave his life, under the bus? Or did that come from someone else? Was it something that was supposed to be off the record and inadvertently included?

As unlikely as it seemed, even small town departments had undercover officers and confidential informants; in a town where everyone was related, or at the very least, screwing each other, it was even more imperative to guard those identities.

What was said about me was largely correct, whether I liked it or not. My personal life *did* seriously interfere with my professional life—screwing Monroe's wife nearly got me killed. But Monroe wouldn't want those details in print.

Rivera's sole purpose was to shake me off the case—and he failed miserably. He was known to meet with police officer Reno Elliot, who intimidated Gina and he was publicly identified as working undercover. Could the connection then be made that Monroe was somehow behind framing Atwater? Much as I hated him, I didn't want to believe Monroe had anything to do with this—and like Barnes, didn't want to be the one to lob accusations at him without any basis. But things were fitting together—and in a way I didn't like. Monroe was stupid enough to use intimidation to keep men away from his idiot wife—but he never struck me as one who would frame someone for murder.

Then, too, maybe he was so worried about who Maris was doing that he didn't know what these two guys were up to.

And why would they—Elliot, Rivera and Monroe, if he was involved—pick on a low-level criminal like Mike Atwater, especially over the death of a sad case like Gina Cantolini? What could she know that would make a police chief nervous—and nervous enough to kill?

The next question: How much of this could I share with Barnes without either compromising Atwater's chances of sailing through the grand jury without an indictment—or getting myself killed?

Mac Brewster said he was going to file his retirement papers before talking to me about what was going on at the FPD. I needed to run him down as well—maybe he was ready to talk this week.

But I had to speak to Barnes first.

"You told me you didn't know who Jorge Rivera was," I said, as soon as he picked up his office phone.

"I couldn't, Fitz! I swear to God! I can't believe that would come out of Monroe's mouth and that an idiot reporter would print something like that! The longer I've had to deal with the *Times* the more I'm convinced they hire idiots and morons. Fucking idiots and morons."

" Monroe ought to know that any time you talk to a reporter it's on the record," I said. "The only other thing I can think is that he told him off the record and the reporter slipped up."

Barnes groaned. "That's going to shoot everything in the ass."

"Everything? What was Rivera involved in?"

"From what I heard, Rivera was providing information on the motorcycle gang Jacob Poole was part of. They were reportedly bringing large quantities of pure heroin into the city, cutting it and selling it."

This was no surprise. Road Anarchy was started by a group of disenchanted Vietnam veterans back when I was a kid. While the club originally provided a place to drink beer and listen to bad local rock bands, as times got harder in F-town, so did the club members, attracting folks like Henson and Poole. The club occasionally had poker runs to raise money for local kids stricken with one horrible disease or another, but as time passed, it became more known for the crimes that allegedly occurred there but could never be proved.

"Jacob Poole? Gina Cantolini's other lover?"

"Yeah. But he didn't kill her, Fitz. We've checked and he's clean—at least where she's concerned."

*****

Ambrosi welcomed me into his stinking office just before lunch.

"Jesus, Fitz, you look like shit." He ran his fingers through his fading comb over and settled back behind the big mahogany desk. "I saw this morning's paper."

"Yeah, I've had better weekends." I dropped into a Morris chair across from him.

Quickly, I filled him in on the shooting and the fire, including what I learned about Rivera.

"So you think the chief of police could be behind this?" Ambrosi's fat cheeks puffed out as he exhaled, a fearful look on his face.

"I don't want to make those sort of allegations unless I've got something more to go on," I said. "But too many things just point his way. I also need to talk to your client to ask him about some information I learned about Gina's family."

Ambrosi scratched the information on a pad of paper. "I've got some time tomorrow afternoon, after two. Meet me at the jail then."

"Another thing—I need someplace to work, since I no longer have an office. Got any empty desks for me?"

Ambrosi wouldn't look me in the eye. "I don't know, Fitz."

"What do you mean, you don't know?" My voice escalated. "I've been hit in the head, shot at, attacked in a parking lot, and my fucking office burned down, all because of *your* client. You don't think that deserves a goddamned desk in a corner here?"

Ambrosi raised his hands, but the fear didn't leave his face. "Calm down, Fitz—you have to understand that I can't put my staff's lives at risk—or my own life, for that matter. We all have families."

"And I don't? Fuck you, Ambrosi. Fuck you and your spineless kind of lawyering. I thought you hired me because you believed your client was innocent. Now, when things start to go balls to the wall, you step back like you're going to let me hang? You afraid of what I'll find out? Huh? *Huh?"*

He colored to the roots of his stringy, thin hair.

"Fuck you, Ambrosi." I turned to go, spinning so quickly pain from the burns on my feet shot straight to my brain.

"Fitz, wait!"

I stopped.

"Let me see if I can find an empty desk for you, OK?"

"You do that."

I left the office—and Gracie's Volvo in Ambrosi's parking lot—walking the four blocks to the jail. Maybe Atwater could take a few minutes away from staring at the ceiling from his jailhouse bunk to talk to me.

He could. After warning him that any conversation he had here would be recorded, the deputy shackled Mike to the floor in front of the scratched Plexiglas window and handed him the phone. He didn't look any worse for wear—the daily jailhouse routine was probably a familiar one for him.

“I’m looking for information on Gina and her family,” I said. “What do you know about her parents?”

Atwater shrugged. “I know her mom lives in North Canton but they don’t like each other. I know her dad is dead, and I know he killed himself. Gina had a sister, but I don’t know who she is.”

“Ever hear the name Mariella?”

“No. Gina’s sister’s name was something else.”

“Like what?”

“Rochelle, maybe? Roxy?”

“You never met her, then.”

Atwater shook his head. “She said her family hated her.”

“Do you know why they hated her?”

“She’d talk about it only when she was really drunk. She said the police thought her dad did something bad to her sister and he committed suicide. Gina said it wasn’t true, though. She tried to tell everybody it wasn’t true, but no one would listen. She always felt really bad about the whole thing, but nobody would admit what they did.”

“What do you mean, ‘admit’?”

“Gina said her mom made up all that stuff about her dad and her sister, but they wouldn’t talk about it. They made her look like she was the crazy one. They cut her out of the family for sticking up for her dad.”

That verified everything Ava Cantolini-Jones had told me. I had one more question.

“Did she ever say where her sister lived?”

“No. I don’t think she knew.”

“OK, thanks.” I nodded.

Back at Gracie’s, I logged on to the laptop, which mercifully came to life with an electronic chime, and found Ava Cantolini-Jones’ phone number. It was about noon in San Francisco and Ava picked up the phone. We exchanged a few pleasantries before getting down to business.

“Mrs. Jones, did your niece Mariella ever go by a different name?”

"After she hit her teens, she wanted to be called by her middle name, so we did. She didn't like the name Mariella, especially since it was an old family name."
"What was her middle name?"

"Rochelle."

Rochelle. Dennis Lance's lush, lavish wife shimmered across my mind and I saw the resemblance between a well-to-do attorney's wife and the body of a dead hooker lying in a casket. Could Rochelle have changed her name? Could she now be Rachel? If anybody had a secret that needed keeping, it would be Mariella Rochelle Cantolini or Rachel Lance, whatever the hell her name was now.

I get it that shit gets said when people get divorced. I get it that kids get dragged into that same shit and they get damaged forever. I don't get it that people take it to the extreme, hanging onto a lie until an innocent man decides to suck on the end of a pistol to make it stop and a young girl is cut out of her family for trying to make it right.

What if Gina somehow found Rachel and threatened to expose her? The woman who had two men fighting over the parentage of her three children had learned long ago how to manipulate people. It wasn't that far a stretch that she would play the same game with her sister.

If what I was thinking was correct, it was particularly important that secret remain so—especially if Rachel's husband wanted to be the next common pleas judge.

And what was the rumor Susan Atwater heard at Gina's funeral, that the prosecutor had paid the bill? *That* made sense now—too much damned sense.

But Rachel didn't react when I called her by her name Saturday night. Was that practice on her part or was I jumping to conclusions?

"Do you happen to have any pictures of Rochelle?"

There was silence on the other end of the line. "Let me look. I'm not sure. Does this have anything to do with Gina's murder?"

"I don't know. I just know that there's an awful lot of people who think I don't need to be investigating Gina's murder, and I'm trying to find out what she knew that pisses so many people off."

We exchanged e-mails and said our goodbyes. It was time for me to go buy flowers and pick up Gracie at work.

I'd need her car again tomorrow: I needed to visit Sharon Hansen. Until I had a picture of Rochelle/Rachel, Mommie Dearest was the next best source I had. I needed to lean on her and lean on her hard.

Chapter 18

The warm sounds of Gracie's cello filled the hallway as I approached her office in the college music department. I stopped outside and laid a hand on the cool wooden door, as if to soak her music into my soul and hold it there forever. I couldn't lose her. I just couldn't. I hoped my plans for the evening, starting with the two-dozen roses I held on my arm and ending with a promise that cleaned out my savings account of all but a couple bucks and change, would bring her back to me forever. The music stopped, and I heard the sound of pages turning—the perfect time to enter.

Gracie was seated near the window, with her cello between her knees, bathed in the spring sunlight, rifling through the sheet music on the stand in front of her. She wore another white gauzy top and camisole, paired today with coral pants and sandals. Sunlight bounced off her hair, held away from her face with a white headband. She looked up and gasped at the flowers.

"Niccolo! You didn't have to do that!" She stood and took them from me, kissing me lightly on one burned cheek. She buried her nose in a bloom and inhaled. "Oh, they smell wonderful."

"Of course I did! How was your day?"

Gracie didn't answer, handing me the flowers back and searching for an empty vase in her coat closet. She stood on tiptoe as she brought one from the back of the shelf, setting it on her desk.

"Pretty good," she said finally. She smiled, I thought a little sadly, as she turned to take the flowers from me and began to arrange them in the vase.

"What happened?"

She shrugged. "I talked to the folks at Berklee College of Music today."

"Oh?"

"I'm not in the running for that job anymore."

"They decided that before even interviewing you?" I hoped I sounded disappointed for her sake. I wanted to jump up and down and cheer.

"Yeah." She cast her eyes down. What did she mean? Did she feel stuck here now? Stuck with me because I wouldn't sign the divorce papers? Was she convinced now that I was ruining her life?

"Well, they don't know what they missed," I said. I wanted to hold her and kiss her forehead, but remembering earlier rebuffs, I stood awkwardly in front of her. "How about we go out to dinner?"

"Sure."

I got the impression I would have gotten the same response if I'd said, "How about we go jump off a bridge?" Or, "Lets go home and burn down the house." At least by the time we got to Ye Olde Gaol, she was starting to smile, though slightly.

After visiting Atwater at the jail earlier today, I'd managed to duck across the street to the Gaol and ask the maître d, Mr. Tony, a fixture at the Gaol for generations, for a slight favor. Of an uncertain age, somewhere between Ma and my oldest brother, Mr. Tony could work wonders for those who came to enjoy an intimate dinner or a grand feast, even on short notice.

Thanks to him, I was able to reserve one of the small corner tables downstairs, where the stony cell walls had been converted to warm intimate little dining areas, with soft lights on the walls and candles on the tables. I didn't want to get one of the small private dining rooms upstairs, mainly because they had windows: the third time could be the charm, if someone still wanted to kill me. I also wanted someplace that had memories, good memories, for both of us.

"Oh, Niccolo!" Gracie swept up a second bouquet of roses from her chair.

We gave Mr. Tony our drink orders and I reached over to take Gracie's hand as we settled into our chairs. She didn't pull away this time.

"You asked me to prove to you that I've changed," I began. "I don't know any other way than to show you. I wanted someplace where it could be just you and me, so I chose the place where I asked the most beautiful woman in the world to marry me six years ago. You know this is the same table we sat at that night."

Gracie looked around and smiled. "Oh, Niccolo," she said again.

Mr. Tony came back with our drinks—a vodka martini for Gracie, a beer for me. He took our dinner orders and left. I took a sip of my beer and began again.

"I know I have a reputation and most of it is well deserved, but you have to know that from the day I met you, I never wanted anyone else. I never looked at another woman. I want you back, Gracie. I want what we had to continue. I want—"

She reached across the table and placed her long graceful fingers on my mouth.

"Hush, Niccolo." Gracie folded her hands around her martini glass. "I have something to tell you. I had a visitor today."

"You did?" *Oh God.*

"Yes. Judy Demyan came by. She saw the article about you in the *Times.*"

"The person who started all this mess came to see you? What did she want?" I turned my pilsner glass in circles on the white tablecloth as I tried to contain my sarcasm.

"That's what she wanted to talk to me about, this whole mess." She looked up at the rough limestone walls. I could see tears cresting in her eyes. "She asked me why you were at your office the night of the fire. I told her that after I'd caught her with you, we'd separated and were probably going to divorce. She got very upset. She told me exactly what happened that day, that she was drunk and angry because her husband had been unfaithful to her and you never encouraged her—the same story you'd always told me. Judy admitted she was out of control and apologized for the whole mess. She feels that she's responsible for your injuries in the fire and she's awfully sorry."

"She should be fucking sorry," I said sharply.

"She's going into rehab."

"Good."

"I owe you an apology, too. I just happened to walk in at exactly the wrong moment and jumped to the conclusion that you'd returned to your old ways, Nicco. That was wrong. If I'd believed you that day, you wouldn't have been in the office the night it was firebombed. You'd have been home with me. You wouldn't have been hurt."

I swallowed hard and slipped my hand into my pocket, wrapping my fingers around the small velvet box there. Gracie kept talking, saying things I never thought I'd hear again.

"I'm not from here, but you are. You grew up here in Fawcettville and I just came here to work. I never experienced the feeling of family that I do with you—you know I come from a long line of Connecticut WASPs whose idea of showing emotion usually involves a credit card. The other night, when you came home from the hospital and your mother made dinner for us, it was just like all those Sundays we had in the past, surrounded by that big, crazy, Italian family of yours. I realized then how much I'd miss it if I let you go." She looked up at the ceiling again and wiped her tears away.

I pulled the velvet box from my pocket. Holding the box in my fist, I opened my mouth to speak, but she held up her hand.

"Not yet, Niccolo. I have a couple more things to tell you. I told you that I'm not in the running for the Berklee College of Music job."

"I know, and I don't want you to feel you're stuck here, Grace, just because they decided you weren't good enough for them," I said. "You're a great musician and an even better teacher—fuck 'em if they don't know what they passed by. I know the college isn't Juilliard, and I know this is a really small town. Six years ago, I asked you to marry me right here at this same table. I brought you here tonight to make a damned good argument for you to take me back and right now, all I can say is this: I want us to continue, and I want you to have this as a promise from me that things will be different from here on out."

"Nicco, honey, you're not listening. I'm the one who called Berklee. I told them I was no longer interested in interviewing for the job. I also called the attorney and withdrew the divorce papers. I want to make things work, too, Niccolo. I want us to work."

She wanted to stay. She wanted to stay *with me.* Wordlessly, I opened the ring box up and sat it on the table between us. She gasped at the band of diamonds.

"I want to start again, too, Gracie," I begged. "I don't ever want to lose you. Please, Gracie. Let's start again."

She took the ring from the box, slipped it onto her finger and nodded.

*****

The two-dozen roses hit the living room floor as the front door slammed behind us. I pushed Gracie up against the closest wall; our lips were locked together, her arms around my neck and my hands frantically tried to open her blouse. She wrapped one long leg around me; my hands left the blouse to grasp her firm, sweet ass.

"Oh God, baby," I whispered into her neck.

"Let's go upstairs," she whispered hoarsely. She shifted her leg back to the floor and ran her hands inside my shirt just as my cell phone rang in the back pocket of my jeans.

"Goddammit," I whispered.

"Don't you *dare* answer that, Niccolo." Her voice was dark and husky.

"Don't worry," I answered, sliding my hands to her breasts and kissing her neck. The phone kept ringing. Gracie pulled the phone out of my pocket, bringing my hips closer to hers. She swept her long hair from her face and held the phone up in front of me.

"Who is this?"

My eyes struggled to focus. My eyes may be telling me I was getting old, but there were other parts that weren't—at least for right now.

"Shit. It's Ambrosi, Mike Atwater's attorney."

"You can call him back later." Her lips met mine as she slid the phone onto a nearby side table. Her hands moved to the front of my jeans and began to work at the zipper. "Right now, we've got better things to do."

*****

About one in the morning, I staggered downstairs for a glass of water. The entry way was bathed in the spring moonlight, making it easy for me to grab the phone from the side table as I passed through to the kitchen. Sitting at the kitchen table, scratching Mozart the cat's ears, I punched in the voicemail code and listened to Ambrosi's message as I sipped from my glass.

"Fitz, it's me. I've got some good news and some bad news. The good news is that I found a desk for you to work from. The other good news is that the time stamp on Jacob Poole's cell phone photo is incorrect. The bad news is Mike Atwater's .38 was finally recovered in the alley behind the Mexican restaurant. Ballistic tests matched it to the weapon that killed Gina and it's got both Mike and Gina's fingerprints on it. I'm thinking we don't have any choice but to work a plea deal after the grand jury. Call me back."

Chapter 19

"You can't just roll over and die because the cops found a weapon!"

The next morning, I kissed a sleeping Gracie goodbye and went to meet Ambrosi.

As promised, he had an office for me, along with keys to the front door. It was one of his back rooms currently empty because of a paralegal out on maternity leave. If the condition of the office was any indication, the paralegal probably took time off for the health of her unborn baby. Like the rest of Ambrosi's offices, it was painted maize yellow, edged brown with the smoke of his cheap cigars where the walls met the ceiling.

There were no windows. Low-watt bulbs gave the room a cave-like aura; I expected to see bats fly out the door when I first flipped the light switch.

The office also stunk from those cigars, the body odor of the losers he perpetually represented and Ambrosi himself. Clearly, I needed to find some new digs for Fitzhugh Investigations, but I couldn't until I finished this case.

Our conversation was held in Ambrosi's large but dingy office. Thank God, the day was warm enough for the window to be opened, sending his cigar stench out the window.

"With his record, my chances of getting him off are even slimmer," Ambrosi whined.

"You can't argue to have prior bad acts excluded? I'm no attorney, but I've watched more than one perp walk because his lawyer argued the fact that he did something once before didn't mean it could be admitted in the current case."

"Not at the grand jury hearing. The fact that he has a long history of domestic violence with the victim will trump that," Ambrosi said.

"What about the time stamp on Poole photo? Could that provide some reasonable doubt?"

"Basically, the picture was taken with a camera with an incorrect time and date stamp on it, then Poole took a photo of that picture with his cell phone," Ambrosi explained. "I'll argue it, but that won't come up until the case comes to court. You know as well as I do, the grand jury is just there to determine whether a crime has been committed, not some mini-rehearsal of the court case. And Gina Cantolini's body is proof a crime was committed."

"You're not giving up on Mike, are you?" I was getting sucked into the cult of Mike Atwater's innocence, even as the evidence kept piling up.

Ambrosi sighed. "One of the first things I say to my clients is 'don't tell me if you're innocent or guilty. Tell me who the witnesses are and I'll tell you if you're innocent or guilty.' I went against my own advice here and it's come back to haunt me."

Ambrosi began ticking off the evidence against his client.

"There's no evidence Jacob Poole had anything to do with the victim's death, despite the photo. We have Mike and Gina arguing at the festival and Officer Reno Elliot breaking up the argument. My client is behind on his child support and the victim told him she wants him to submit to a DNA test because there's a good possibility the boys he thinks are his son belong to someone else. There is the gun, which is registered to my client, which matches the bullets found in the victim's chest. Maybe I could bargain it down to life."

"Hold on! Jorge Rivera was about to tell me that the victim had information that made a lot of people nervous. He told me the same folks who wanted me off the case because they knew the shit would hit the fan if I found out," I countered. "Rivera was rumored to be working undercover with the police to investigate the heroin Poole's motorcycle gang brings into Fawcettville. I've been cold cocked, shot at and had my office blown up investigating this case. That's too much effort being put into getting some low-level criminal convicted in the death of a drunken hooker. There's something more here, Jim, and we can't give up yet."

Ambrosi shrugged. "I have my doubts, Fitz."

"So why would somebody try to kill me, particularly twice in one night? You got any answers for that?"

He shook his head. "No, I don't. You've pissed a lot of people off through the years, Fitz."

"Now hold on! Everybody wants to blame Chief Monroe, but that shit was seven years ago. I wish the people in this town would forget things like that. I made a mistake and I had to retire from the force because of it," I said. "Don't get me wrong—Nathaniel Monroe is a dick and shouldn't be chief. If he'd dump that idiot slut he's married to, a lot of his problems would end. For all of that, I don't think Monroe is trying to kill me."

Ambrosi lit one of his stinking cigars and drew the smoke deep into his lungs, but didn't speak. Was he just too spineless to say anything? Or did he know something I didn't?

"I'm going to Canton today. I've got a hunch I need to follow."

"Be careful out there, Fitz. Just be careful."

*****

I parked Gracie's Volvo down the block and walked back to examine Sharon Hansen's house.

The North Canton neighborhood around the house was genteel and quietly polished. No one's yard showed signs of a single weed; the cars in the driveway were Lincolns, Volvos and Cadillacs, uniformly expensive and clean. The streets still retained their bricks, installed during the Great Depression. Down the block, a historical marker in the grass between the sidewalk and the street marked the home of a local writer who made his name concocting novels of the Old West and the Civil War.

These houses were old, but weren't anything like you'd find in Fawcettville, in New Tivoli or Tubman Gardens. Here, social status spread like chlamydia down the well-appointed hallways and through tasteful living rooms and, like all new money, you worked hard to keep it that way.

Sharon's house, which sat on the corner of Northwest Princeton and East Yale streets, was painted white with tasteful green shutters at each window. A low, brick wall began at the sidewalk, shoring up its small, sloping front yard where daffodils bloomed along the edge. A white Lexus was parked in the driveway.

The front door faced East Yale Street and had two columns on either side. From around the corner, I could see a sleeping porch on the second floor that had brightly colored outdoor furniture. If Sharon were as ill as she claimed to be in our phone conversation, she could sit there for morning coffee and look over her immaculately groomed back yard.

I walked up the concrete steps to the front door and knocked. Inside, I heard purposeful steps on wooden floors. The lock turned and a woman opened the red front door.

No wonder Brian Cantolini felt blessed when she turned her attentions to him: Sharon Hansen was stunning. Fit and petite, her blonde hair was tastefully styled; she wore a peach colored twinset and tapered tan pants. Her face was remarkably unwrinkled, but steely, and her makeup perfect. A matching tan purse was on her arm, like she was ready to leave.

"May I help you?" she asked.

I could see equal parts of both her and Brian in their daughter Gina's face—and another face, one from Saturday night's symphony benefit.

"Sharon Hansen? You look remarkably well for someone who was in a wheelchair just last week."

"Excuse me?"

"I'm Niccolo Fitzhugh of Fitzhugh Investigations. I talked to you last week about your daughter Gina's death. You said you weren't able to attend her funeral because you were ill and in a wheelchair. It looks like you've made a complete recovery."

Sharon tried to slam the door, but I caught it with my shoulder, muscling my way into her foyer. I grabbed her by the arm.

"Get your hands off me! You leave here right now or I'll call the police!" she said.

"I don't think so. I know the truth behind why your husband committed suicide. I think it's tied to your daughter's death and you're going to tell me why."

Sharon shook her arm free. "I have no idea what you are talking about."

"Don't lie to me," I said, grabbing her arm again. I pulled her close to my face, just to watch her squirm. "I know you accused your late husband of sexually abusing your daughter Mariella ten years ago. You talked your daughter into believing he'd done it—or you both made up this story to get something out of a man who worked hard to provide for you and your spoiled little brat. But it got out of control, didn't it? The school board got hold of it, then the police got hold of it and you two were just in too deep to admit you'd lied, right?"

Light footsteps, like a woman's, sounded on the linoleum in the kitchen, just off the dining room to my right.

"Mom? Who was that?" A voice called out. "We need to get going!"

I jerked Sharon's arm.

"You tell Mariella or Rochelle or Rachel or whatever name she goes by these days there's someone here to see her," I hissed.

Sharon stared back at me, her eyes hard.

I glanced past her to see Rachel Lance peek from around the kitchen doorframe. Her pink lipstick was perfect and her clothing casual in a way that screamed how much work it took to just throw something on. Her makeup was more natural, less striking, but her face was still beautiful. Her big, brown, Italian eyes were ringed with heavy black lashes; they got even bigger as she recognized me.

"Rochelle!" Sharon called. *"Run!"*

The kitchen door slammed. I dropped Sharon's arm and ran to the kitchen, then out the back door as Rachel backed down the drive in her white Lexus. The tires squealed on the brick road as she sped off down the street.

I didn't follow her—there was no need. I would catch up to her later. I walked back into the foyer, where Sharon Hansen stood, shaking, and her perfectly manicured hands over her mouth. I grabbed the sleeve of her sweater and she gasped.

"Tell me the truth about what you did to Gina," I demanded. "I know you pushed her away when she tried to stand up for her father and tell everyone you were lying. You're the reason she was an addict. You're the reason why she sold her body to pay for her drugs and her booze. You're behind why she couldn't tell which loser she slept with was the father of her children."

"Stop it! You don't understand!" Sharon turned her face away from me in tears. I jerked the sleeve of her sweater again and she cried out in fear.

"I don't have to understand, Mrs. Hansen. I'm the one who used to pick Gina up when she was a drunken, homeless teenager on the streets. I'm the one who arrested her for prostitution, and now I'm the one who's been hired to find out how she really died."

I brought my face close to hers. She raised her hand up, as if to protect herself from a blow.

"Please, please! You're scaring me," she cried.

"Just tell me one thing," I said. "You couldn't be enough of a mother to attend your own daughter's funeral.

Are you also cold enough to make someone else pay the bill?"

"No! I sent a check as soon as Rachel told me, but I mailed it. I didn't let Dennis drop it off. I'm not that stupid, Mr. Fitzhugh."

I let go of Sharon's arm and she sank against the foyer wall.

"Does your son-in-law know his wife's real name?"

Sharon shook her head. "After Brian killed himself and I got remarried, Rochelle didn't want to be known by her birth name. She was embarrassed at all the attention she got when the trial was over and people learned what her last name was. So, Joe adopted her and she legally changed her name to Rachel Hansen. She met Dennis in grad school, when he was teaching a business law class. They've only been married a couple years."

" Did she ever tell him the truth?"

"I don't know," Sharon whispered. "I never asked."

"Tell me how Gina died. Tell me everything you know," I demanded.

"I don't know how she died. I only know Rachel got back in contact with her sister recently. I just know she wouldn't kill her sister. She's got too much to lose."

"Did it ever cross your mind she might have killed her because she's got too much to hide?"

Chapter 20

Mac Brewster texted me as I drove back from North Canton: "Meet me at Horvath's coffee shop. Friday was my last day—I can talk now."

It wasn't a convenient time. No doubt Rachel Lance—or whatever the hell her name was—was racing back to her prosecutor husband, probably to tell him I broke into the house and assaulted her mother.

I'd have to deal with her later. Things were starting to fall together and I didn't like what I was seeing.

I had no idea if Rachel/Rochelle was a first or second wife. Public folks like Dennis Lance always managed to keep their private lives hidden behind a curtain that only opened when they wanted it to be, trotting family members out at election time as little vote-getting minions. If Rachel was a second or even third wife, he'd managed something I seldom saw: A civilized divorce. There was no angry female around town who ranted and raved about what a bastard Dennis Lance was—and God knows, of all people, I would have heard it.

As I drove east on Highway 30, I began to think. Whatever scenario I came up with, I couldn't figure out who moved the body. How did they, if it was more than one person, dump a body in the middle of town, particularly during a festival?

Where did Jorge Rivera come into play in all this? Did Rachel hire him to scare me off? Or did Dennis? He would be the one who had inside knowledge on who was investigating the case. Could he have made an inadvertent slip during dinner conversation that started Rachel in search of an enforcer? And how was Rivera somehow tied to the police force?

If Dennis had no idea of his wife's own questionable past, its exposure would certainly derail his campaign. Here he was, married to a woman who perjured herself ten years ago, who accused her father of sexual abuse so graphic it stunned the jurors and led directly to Brian Cantolini's suicide.

What if Dennis knew about it? What if it was Dennis Lance who killed Gina to get rid of a very uncomfortable liability?

He knew enough about the lowlifes in this town and could easily tie someone else to the murder. A police chief who was looking for every reason to keep his job might know just who to accuse, too. Someone who didn't matter, someone who was a loser, whose life was as much of a waste as Gina Cantolini and who's family didn't have the money to pay for a high-powered defense lawyer... someone like Mike Atwater.

But again, who put the body under the festival stage? Everyone would recognize Dennis Lance walking through the center of town, and knowing Lance, he couldn't leave a burning building without shaking a potential voter's hand first.

Hmmm. Some of it could be possible, but some of it just didn't make sense.

If Rachel killed Gina, or if Dennis Lance did it, it didn't fit that either one of them moved the body. There had to be a third person, but whom?

I slowed the Volvo down as I came to the edge of Fawcettville. Maybe Mac Brewster could put some of these questions to rest.

*****

Brewster was sitting at the back of the coffee shop when I arrived, eating a *zserbó*, three layers of sweet dough, filled with raspberry jam, ground pecans, and coated in dark chocolate.

I ordered a cup of coffee along with a box of half a dozen apricot *kiflis* to take home to Gracie, and joined Brewster.

"So how does it feel to be set free from the work-a-day world?" I asked.

Brewster smiled as he attacked his *zserbó* with his fork. "You ever have one of these things? Great God Almighty, they are good. I haven't felt this relaxed in years, Fitz—*years.*"

"Well, I'll tell you right now that you'll get bored soon and you'll be looking for something to fill your days. I did at any rate. That's how I ended up in this business."

"Already got a job—head of security at the college. Regular hours and decent pay and everything. I just couldn't stay at the FPD anymore, Fitz. Just couldn't do it."

"Tell me everything you know about Jorge Rivera. You probably heard about my little incident."

"Yeah, you sure manage to attract the shit, don't you?" Brewster took a sip of his coffee. "From what I hear, the chief told that reporter off the record that Rivera was a CI, and it somehow got into the story. Monroe was pissed, called the editor and everything."

"I heard Rivera was working with the police to provide information about Jacob Poole and that motorcycle gang he's part of. They're supposedly bringing heroin into town."

Brewster shook his head. "He wasn't working with the police. That whole thing isn't in local hands at all. He was working with the feds."

"The feds?"

Brewster took another bite of his pastry and nodded. "We all knew about the operation, but those CI's were all tapped by the feds, not anyone who could be recognized here in town. He couldn't have been very good. The last two or three buys Rivera set up fell through, from what I heard. Why?"

"Rivera was hired to shake me off the case—he told me so. After Ambrosi hires me to investigate Gina Cantolini's death, Rivera starts following me around. The first time I visited Atwater at the jail, Rivera caught me coming out of my office and knocked me out cold. I catch him looking up at my office window with binoculars. I go to meet Jacob Poole at Lupe's restaurant and he's waiting for me outside. We get into it in the alley, he gets away from me and I hear a gunshot, but can't find a body."

"You're kidding me."

"No, Mac! I checked at the hospital and everything. The next time Rivera takes a run at me, it's in the parking lot at Memorial Hall, Saturday night. I get the best of him—again—and he tells me the powers that be want me off this case, but won't give me a name. We meet at Puccini's, he's about to tell me who's behind all this and the poor sumbitch gets shot in the head."

"Then your office gets firebombed that same night? You sure manage to wade right into it, Fitz." Brewster shook his head.

"Here's what I want to know. Barnes seems to think that the bullet Rivera took and the firebombing was meant for me—and that it came from someone connected with the police department. Someone high up."

"I think Detective Barnes is wrong." Brewster was serious.

I shrugged. "I think so, too, Mac. For all the mistakes I made in the past, the last thing I'm going to do is go sniffing around Maris again. I'm happily married now, Mac. I'm not going to jeopardize that. And Monroe, well—"

"We all know the story of how Lt. Baker saved your bacon that night. Monroe knows not to go after you anymore. He's been on thin ice too long. He has no decision-making power these days, outside of signing expense reports and filling in duty rosters. The big stuff, that's all been shifted to the city manager. All Monroe does is sit in his office and try to figure out who his wife is sleeping with now. That's why things are so crazy. I've heard the city manager has a drawer full of resumes of guys who want to be the new chief. The prosecutor has been the one who's been working with the feds on this heroin investigation."

My ears perked up at that one. "Dennis Lance has been working with the feds?"

"Yeah. I mean, he's not involved in daily operations, but he's aware, you know? Why?"

"I owe you, Mac. This time I really owe you."

Chapter 21

I paid for Brewster's coffee and pastry and headed out to the car. I had a few hours before I needed to pick up Gracie—time enough to do a little snooping.

I called Alicia Linnerman from the Volvo.

"Hello, Fitz," she purred. "How's every little thing? Feeling better?" She apparently had gotten over the bruises Elliot gave her and was ready to move on.

"Great. Gracie and I are back together. Hey, is your boss around?"

"Sure." She sounded crestfallen. "I can connect you."

"Wait! I don't want to speak to Lance. I need his home address," I said.

"What for?"

"Let's say I'm seeking a moment of clarity."

"His address is a matter of public record, Fitz. You could find it."

"I'm in the car. Help a guy out."

Linnerman sighed and gave me the address.

I wanted to sound like Sam Spade in *The Maltese Falcon*, the way he talked to his secretary, Effie Perrine. I wanted to say "You're a good girl, Effie," but Alicia would have been more than offended. She probably would have sent Sadie the mastiff after my ass. Instead, I just said, "Thanks. If I need more, I'll call you back."

"Whatever." She hung up.

Like everything else in this damn case, I was headed the wrong direction. I made a U-turn in the middle of the street and headed out into the country.

*****

The house was an old red brick farmhouse, with hunter green shutters and colorful pots of petunias hanging along white porch rails traveling along the front and east side of the house. It was an older home, brought back to life with a lot of restoration work: the bricks looked recently sandblasted and the roof had to be new, or at least recent because it matched the green shutters. A brick walkway, accented with marigolds popping out of fresh, dark mulch, curved a couple times on its way to the gravel driveway, which was edged with box hedges.

The bank barn behind the house showed pieces of younger, yellow wood newly nailed in place and a fresh reddish paint was creeping up the exterior walls. White vinyl fencing extended from the backside of the barn down to the road, providing a paddock for Lance's prize horses, which grazed on uniformly level and uniformly green grass.

Renovation was still continuing, apparently. A contractor's truck and a construction Dumpster sat in the wide graveled area between the house and the barn, next to a gooseneck horse trailer and gleaming white pick-up truck. Rachel Lance's white Lexus was just visible behind the Dumpster.

From my vantage point at the end of the drive, I lowered my binoculars and pondered my scenario.

Had Rachel contacted her husband on her way home from her mother's? Did he have any clue of what happened today?

As I tried to put everything together, a muscular construction worker walked out, carrying a bank of kitchen cabinets, which he tossed into the Dumpster like it was nothing. He had on a flannel shirt with the sleeves ripped partially off and his dirty jeans had holes in the knees. His beard was dirty blonde and scraggly, down to the middle of his beefy chest. He wore a blue construction helmet that covered the upper half of his face.

Was that a bandage around one arm? I wonder what happened? That had to be hard to work injured, I mused. My burns weren't yet healed, but I was feeling better. Making love to Gracie had been exquisite, of course, but it still involved some gymnastics to keep pain at bay. I can't imagine redoing some spoiled housewife's kitchen while injured.

I raised the binoculars to my eyes as the same construction worker returned to the Dumpster with another bank of cabinets. He stopped and folded his beefy arms, staring at the Volvo. Adjusting the binoculars, I got a closer look at the bandage. The wound wasn't professionally dressed; the gauze was haphazardly applied and covered somewhat with an elastic bandage, held in place by a safety pin. A single circle of blood leached through the brown elastic bandage.

Whatever happened to this guy's arm, he hadn't sought professional medical care—which likely meant it happened in the commission of a felony.

Catching a glimpse of the tattoos across his knuckles, I dropped the binoculars and threw the car into reverse. It was Charlie Horton, the thug who said he attended the Saturday night birthday party for Poole's daughter. Suddenly I knew where the wound on his arm came from: it was a bullet wound, fired in the alley behind Lupe's. Horton had tailed Rivera to Lupe's and gotten shot for his trouble.

Had I just been recognized? It didn't matter. I would be back soon—and when I did, I would have the answers I'd been looking for.

*****

Gracie was waiting outside the music department building, her arm draped around her cello case like a lover when I pulled into the parking lot. The cello went into the back seat before she slid into the passenger seat next to me. I handed her the box of Hungarian pastries.

"Sweets for my sweet," I said.

"Ooh! Thanks! So how was your day?" She kissed me before I could answer. Her lips were warm and soft; I resisted the temptation to slide my hands up her skirt or into her blouse. That could wait until we got home.

"I'm getting close on the Atwater case, I think," I finally said, putting the car into gear and pulling into traffic. "I might need to go out tonight."

"Maybe I don't want to know, then." She smiled a little wryly and put her hand on my leg.

"Do we still have the security system at the house?" It was one thing I'd insisted on when I moved into Gracie's house six years ago. Cops live with a particular paranoia; we've put away enough people and dealt with enough scumbags to know one day they'll get out and they just might come looking to hurt us—or someone we love. And just because I wasn't on the force anymore didn't mean shit: I worried even more now. I never slept without my Glock in reach and, until my Kahr burned in the fire, never went anyplace without more than one weapon just for that reason.

Gracie shot me a sidelong glance, but didn't answer.

"Don't tell me you canceled it," I said slowly.

"Of course, I didn't cancel it," Gracie said. "You've made me damned near as paranoid as you are."

"*Gracie...*It's not paranoia. It's self preservation." I turned the corner and pulled into the body shop parking lot. My Excursion was ready to go, its new black paint job glistening in the sun. I slipped from the driver's seat as she walked around the Volvo.

"You don't think I can take care of myself? That I need some *man* around to keep poor, little me safe and sound?" I couldn't tell if she was being sarcastic or funny as she snatched the Volvo keys from my hand.

"That's not what I'm saying, not at all. These situations aren't anything like your fencing meets. If somebody breaks into the house—"

"I'll be *fine*, Niccolo. Don't worry."

"I hope so. I've got one place more I need to stop. It might be a little bit."

"Don't be too long." She slipped into the Volvo and started the engine. I leaned in through the driver's window and kissed her goodbye. A look of uncertainty crossed her face, replaced quickly by a brash smile.

"I won't be. I've got all this to come home to."

*****

After a dinner, we curled up on the couch to watch some PBS show Gracie loved. Comfortable in jeans and T-shirt, she seemed a little more at ease, snuggled against my shoulder. As the sun began to set and the TV show slogged on, I got antsy—too antsy, apparently.

"You're not fooling anybody, Niccolo. Stop checking your damned cellphone."

"I'm sorry."

She sat up, folded her arms and stared at the TV. We sat in silence until my phone finally buzzed.

"You ready?" I asked my caller. "Where should I meet you? OK, give me fifteen minutes. I'll be there. Bye."

"So, where are you headed?" She tried to sound casual, but distrust brimmed in her dark eyes. I looked over to see her trying to stare at the television, her brown eyes filled with conflict. I touched her arm.

"Gracie. Honey. Remember? You said you were going to trust me."

She twisted the band of diamonds I'd just given her.

"Come back to me, Niccolo. Come back to me in one piece."

*****

Alicia Linnerman was waiting at the door of her apartment when I pulled up.

"Barnes is already here," she said, closing the door behind me. I heard Sadie barking from the bedroom. "A couple patrol officers are here, too—they're all back in the kitchen."

"Where's Dennis?"

"Working late, putting his argument together for Friday's grand jury," Alicia said over her shoulder as I followed. "Don't worry, one of the other prosecutors working with him is supposed to call if he leaves. Usually, a couple days before a big case, he stays at the office until at least ten at night, running through the evidence. I've seen him do it enough times in the past year, so we should be fine."

Barnes was sitting at the kitchen

table, making circles of condensation on Alicia's table with his iced tea glass.The uniformed officers leaned against the kitchen counter. The wire I was going to wear, along with the battery pack and a roll of surgical tape sat across from him on the table. I took off my jacket and began to unbutton my shirt.

"You know, I wouldn't have believed all this a week ago until you called me this afternoon, Fitz," he said.

"Until he stopped by my office, I wouldn't have either, " Alicia said. "There are just too many connections to Gina Cantolini to not look into them. I hate to think that my boss is involved in any of this."

Silence hung over the apartment kitchen as the patrol officers went to work, taping the wire to my chest. If my theory was right, Michael Atwater might walk free but Rachel Lance—and possibly the prosecutor himself—could be facing murder charges. Things were fucked up enough in F-Town and I was about to make them worse.

And what if I was wrong? Gracie would be sorry she bowed out of the Berklee job hunt because we couldn't live in Fawcettville any longer.

As soon as they were done, I put my shirt back on.

Alicia signaled toward her front door. "Lets do this." She grabbed my arm as everybody filed out to the sidewalk.

"Fitz, wait a minute," she said. "I need to tell you something." She tipped her face up toward mine.

"What?"

"Dr. Darcy is a very lucky woman."

I smiled at her. "And I'm a very lucky man."

"Yeah, you are." Alicia was silent for a moment. "We could have been something, Fitz. We really could have." She patted me on the arm.

"There might have been a time when I thought the same thing, but not now. I got a second chance, Alicia. I can't let that go."

"I know. You be careful out there. I don't want to be the reason you don't come home to her."

*****

Barnes and the two uniforms parked in the surveillance van at the end of the driveway, along the side of the road. A sheriff's cruiser would be in the area if this whole thing went south. I parked behind them and leaned in the window to talk to Barnes, who was sitting in the passenger seat.

"You think I did a shitty job investigating this, don't you, Fitz?"

"No, I don't. All the evidence pointed to Mike Atwater. Until this afternoon, it did."

"We'll be listening. When you get what we need, we'll move in."

"And if I don't?"

Barnes shrugged. "We're fucked and Mike Atwater gets indicted Friday."

The kitchen light at Lance's farmhouse shone onto the gravel beside the house as I pulled up. Rachel Lance peeked out the side window.

Her mouth fell open when I stepped from the Excursion, and she flipped the curtains closed.

I pounded on the kitchen door. "Open the door, Rachel," I called out. "My name is Niccolo Fitzhugh, Fitzhugh Investigations. I know you're Gina Cantolini's sister. I know you have information on her murder."

The door lock clicked and she slowly opened the door a crack.

"Go away."

"I want to know why your secret is so important you'd let an innocent man go to prison for a murder he didn't commit."

"I said go away. I have nothing to say to you."

I leaned in to glare at half of the beautiful face peeking at me from behind the door. Even wearing T-shirt and sweats, Rachel Lance still looked expensive; without makeup, the resemblance to her dead sister was striking.

Both girls, in fact, had a marked similarity to Sharon Hansen, the woman who started this whole downward spiral. She was directly responsible for Brian's suicide and, by pushing her youngest daughter into a life of drugs and alcohol, indirectly responsible for Gina's death. Too bad she would never face punishment for anything—at least not in this world.

"You can live with the fact a man could be put to death for something you're responsible for?"

"I said, I have nothing to say to you."

I lowered my shoulder and pushed my way in the door. Rachel gasped as she staggered backward against a contractor's ladder in the middle of the room.

The kitchen was torn up, down to the exterior brick walls in a couple places. New walls were framed up and we stood on a wooden subfloor. There were no appliances, except for a microwave oven and a coffee pot on a folding table. A container of Chinese take-out, disposable wooden chopsticks and a greasy paper plate sat next to the microwave.

"Sit down." I pointed to the pair of folding chairs next to the table. "I'm not playing games with you. I'm serious. You're going to tell me every fucking thing that happened that night, and you're going to do it now."

Rachel ran her hands through her shoulder-length hair, and took a moment to get her thoughts together. She didn't seem like the slinky siren I'd seen Saturday at the benefit. She was anything but the unattainable goddess tonight. Tonight, she looked like someone whose painful choices kept her up too many nights in a row.

"You don't understand—"

"I don't, Rachel? Or is it Rochelle? Or Mariella? You're very lucky the statute of limitations has run out on perjury on your little performance ten years ago."

"You don't know what it's like to live with what I've done. I tried to make it up to Gina. I did! I gave her money, I tried to get her a job, I even tried to get her into rehab, but she wouldn't go."

"I imagine your meetings couldn't have been pleasant."

Rachel turned her head away and didn't speak. I kept pushing.

"You didn't know how much of a mess murder makes, did you? Is that the reason you tore the kitchen up, to get rid of the bloodstains? How about I have the cops come test the contents of that Dumpster out back? A little Luminol would turn up the blood stains on those cabinets."

"Stop it!" she screamed. "It wasn't supposed to happen at all! But I didn't do it! You have to believe me!"

"Tell me the whole story."

"It wasn't bad at first, but then she started just showing up here at the house. She always wanted money or groceries or something. Jorge Rivera—"

"Jorge Rivera works for you?" Things were starting to fit together now.

"Yes, Jorge is my farm laborer. He saw Gina and asked me how I knew her and that he knew her. That scared me. I couldn't let her keep coming here—somebody might talk."

"Helping your sister is OK as long as she doesn't publicly acknowledge that you're related. I understand." I couldn't control my sarcasm.

"That's not it at all. It was her boyfriend, that, that Jacob Poole guy—he was dangerous. I didn't want him coming to the house, either."

"So tell me what really happened."

"I never knew when she was going to show up. It got bad—she would be drunk or high, but always agitated somehow. She wouldn't sit still. She'd wander all over the house when she came and I had to follow her. I wanted to count the silverware after she left, you know?"

"No, I don't."

Rachel's story was building momentum. She ignored my snide comments and kept going.

"Two weeks before she was killed, she came over here, scared to death. She told me Poole was bringing heroin into town, that he was cutting up for sale at her house and she was scared she'd lose her kids. She'd put locks on the outside of their bedroom doors so they wouldn't just happen to come downstairs after she put them to bed. I told her that she needed to go to the police with that garbage. What if the house caught on fire? 'Oh, the police won't help me—they're as crooked as everyone else in this town,' she said. 'I got one cop comes to the house, wanting sex and shit. When I don't give it to him, he beats me.' "

"Officer Reno Elliot?"

"She never said who it was. I just know between Jacob, her addiction and the cop she felt trapped, with no way out. She had another boyfriend—"

"My client, Michael Atwater."

"Yes. She would talk about him, sometimes. He kept trying to get her away from Jacob Poole, but I think she knew he wouldn't be much better. She kept him hanging on, though. She had him convinced her two boys were his, then Jacob Poole's family demanded a paternity test and things got out of control."

I thought about the picture of all the red-haired Atwater men Susan had shown me. Innocent as he may be, Michael Atwater was still one dumb shit.

"So what happened the day she was killed?"

"It was late afternoon—Dennis was working at the festival, Jorge was in the barn and I was here by myself when Gina came over here. She was angry and high, waving this pistol around. She'd argued with Michael over the DNA thing. Jacob told her he thought he had informants in the motorcycle club, and she accused me of telling Dennis about the heroin operation."

Rachel stopped for a moment and clasped her hands over her mouth. She was shaking.

"Let me finish the story for you. She'd heard your husband was going to run for judge and, since she thought you'd exposed the heroin operation, threatened to tell the world what particularly disgusting kind of perjury her dear, darling older sister once committed in a court of law."

Rachel's denials filled the room, but I ignored her. I was too angry, angry that Rachel's efforts to help Gina came not from sisterly concern or an effort to reconcile what she had done, but to keep the lies and the secrecy going.

"I'll bet the gun Gina brought with her was a .38, the same gun registered to my client. You two argued, then got into a fight, didn't you? You choked her, but she was stronger than you thought. People get awfully strong when someone is trying to kill them, don't they, Rachel? They're even stronger when they're high on something. Gina pointed the gun at you, didn't she?"

The denials stopped.

"I'm on to something, aren't I? She turned the gun on you, and you managed to get it pointed back at her, didn't you?"

"No!"

"Don't bullshit me. You struggled, you turned the gun toward her and it went off. You killed your sister, Mariella Cantolini—you killed her because she was going to expose you and you couldn't take that, could you?"

"OK, we struggled, but I never put my hands on her neck. That was Jacob. Jorge saw her pull up and called him to say she was here. They both burst in here and Jorge held me back while Jacob grabbed Gina by the neck and beat her head against the cabinets until she dropped the gun. Oh, God, it was awful!" Rachel began to sob.

"What happened next?"

"She was unconscious when he dragged her out of here—he took the gun with him, too. There was blood everywhere! I didn't know until the next day he'd shot her."

"You didn't think to call the police? You didn't think he was going to kill her?"

"I-I couldn't! I was so scared!"

"So scared you decided to suddenly remodel the kitchen?"

"No!" Rachel sobbed, but I wasn't finished.

"Who hired Rivera to chase me off the case?"

"I did," she said, through her tears. "Rivera was as frightened as I was about Gina's murder. He came back to the house the next day and told me Poole shot her. I told him we both could face charges if the truth came out. Dennis told me you were investigating the case and I told Rivera he had to do anything he could to scare you off. Dennis said Ambrosi was a burnout and you were a has-been loser as a cop. I figured it wouldn't be hard." For a moment, arrogance flitted across her face.

"You figured wrong." I could barely contain my anger. "Thanks to you, two people are dead, my office was destroyed and I got to spend the night in the hospital. All because your sister threatened to expose you and ruin everything you've worked so hard to hide. OK boys, I think we've got everything we need."

"You're wearing a wire? This has been recorded? Oh my God! My life is ruined!" She burst into tears as Barnes and the two uniforms came through the door.

I watched as Barnes handcuffed and Mirandized a hollow-eyed Rachel.
Barnes hit her with every charge he could think of. She would face tampering charges, obstruction of justice and possibly even accessory to murder charges, all to cover a lie told in her parents' nasty divorce long ago.

Barnes put his hand on her head as she slid into the back of the sheriff's cruiser.

"One more question, Rachel." I leaned into cruiser. "Dennis doesn't know you were born a Cantolini, does he?"
She shook her head. "No. I never told him."
"Why not?"

"By the time I met Dennis, I'd reconciled with my mother and my stepfather adopted me, even though I was an adult. I didn't see the need to tell him the truth at first. I wanted to hide from what I'd done."

"And you'd done more than your share, didn't you?"

"I was young and stupid and all I saw was black and white, OK? My dad had a girlfriend and I was devastated. I got back at him the only way I knew how."

"What changed your attitude?"

"I fell in love with a married man."

"Dennis Lance was married when you met him?" I could almost hear the smirk break across Barnes' face.

She turned her head away. "Yes. The marriage was in shambles and they both knew it. They'd been separated for years, but that doesn't mean his first wife wasn't pissed off when she found out."

"But she didn't run out and accuse him of sexually abusing the kids, did she? She didn't cost him his career or his life, did she?"

She was silent for a moment. "No."

"That's how civilized people do it, Rachel. They keep the kids out of the middle of it and they work it out." Spitting gravel, an FPD cruiser screamed up the drive and came to a sharp stop as we walked out to the gravel driveway.

Chief Monroe stepped from the cruisers. Everybody froze. I took a deep breath. The bastard wouldn't shoot me now, would he? I slipped my right hand into my jacket and touched my Glock.

"You need to get home, Fitz," Chief said. "There's been a shooting at your house."

"What*?*' I asked.

This time, Monroe wasn't a prick. He was professional. He might have wanted to kill me at one time, but not tonight, not now. There was concern in his eyes, real honest to God concern. My heart sank to my feet. *Not Gracie. Anybody but Gracie.*

"From what the officers on scene are telling me, your wife shot an intruder, one Jacob Poole. We're still investigating, but as I understand it, there were several shots fired. That's all I know right now."

"Is she OK?"

I didn't wait for his answer. I jumped into the Excursion and sped down the Lance's driveway.

Chapter 22

Don't let it be Gracie. Don't let it be Gracie.

The roads back to Fawcettville were dark and mercifully empty as I pushed the accelerator to the floor on my way back to town. Gracie and I had been together too long and our path to reconciliation probably still had some bumps to come. It just couldn't come to an end now, simply because of this case.

I would kill Jacob Poole with my bare hands if he did anything, *anything* to my wife.

Police cruisers surrounded the house as I slammed the Excursion into park and jumped from the car. The EMTs were loading a gurney into the back of the ambulance as I ran toward it. A patient was wrapped in white blankets and surrounded by police—I couldn't see who it was.

"Hey! Wait!"

A police officer—some kid I didn't recognize, much less look old enough to be issued a service revolver—stopped me from coming closer.

"I'm sorry, sir, but—"

"Is that my wife? Tell me that's not my wife!" I grabbed the young cop by the shoulders.

"Calm down, calm down. Your wife is Grace Darcy?"

"Is she OK? Is that her?" I pointed at the ambulance. One of the surrounding cops latched the back doors closed and pounded on the door, a signal for the driver to turn on the lights and sirens and scream down the street toward medical care. The young cop turned me away the house and toward one of the cruisers.

God, don't let her be dead. Don't let her be dead.
He opened a rear door and indicated I should sit down. I'd spent twenty years on one side of these situations, calming family members in crisis. Now, I was the one sitting in the back of the cruiser, waiting for news that would either make everything OK or ruin my whole life.

Don't let Gracie be hurt. Don't let her be shot.
It couldn't end this way. I finally had the woman of my dreams and my life was beginning to come around to the way it should be. I couldn't lose Gracie, not now, not this way. If I did, Jacob Poole would suffer excruciatingly for anything he did to her.
The cop spoke into the microphone on his shoulder and turned back to me.

"She's in the house, talking with a detective. I don't know if she suffered any injuries, but if she did, they're minor. I let them know you're—"
"She's injured? My wife is injured?" I pushed my way out of the cruiser, past the cop and into the house.

Eyes red from crying, Gracie sat at the kitchen table, clutching her hands together nervously, talking to Det. Paul Barani. Barani had been a sergeant when I left the force. He was a good man, thorough, and less of a burnout than Barnes. Like Barnes, he was tall and skinny, like there was some sort of caloric restriction that came with the job. Like Brewster, he'd kept himself as far as possible from the drama of Maris Monroe.

A .22-caliber Lady Smith and Wesson with a pink grip sat in the middle of the table; in one corner, small amounts of Poole's blood spattered around the lower kitchen cabinets and onto the floor. There was a bit of blood spatter on Gracie's jeans.

Thank God, she was just fine. Gracie was OK.

"Oh God, Nicco!" She rushed into my arms.

"It's OK, baby. It's OK," I whispered into her hair as I clasped her tightly. "I'm here. It's over." I took her face in my hands to check for injuries. Seeing none, I kissed her forehead and tried to smooth her hair.

"He came through the kitchen window and set off the alarm," Gracie, normally brassy and tough, shook as she spoke. "I was still in the living room watching TV. I jumped up when I heard him—"

"Where was the gun?"

"In between the seat cushion and the arm of the couch. I usually keep it in the drawer by my side of the bed, but after you left tonight, I had a bad feeling, so I got up and stuffed it down where I could get it. He came at me, I screamed, I pulled out the gun..." She struggled as tears rolled down her cheeks. "And I shot him."

"You did the right thing. You're OK—that's the most important thing." I pulled her closer.

"Hello, Fitz." Barani reached out to shake my hand. "We tried to get her to go to the hospital, just to get checked out, but she refused. She wouldn't go until you got here. She's a damned good shot, by the way. Got him in the thigh. May have hit something big, from all the blood. She had him cornered here in the kitchen by the time we got here."

"After I shot him once, he tried to get up again and attack me. I put one in the wall to show him I was serious."

"I'm sure he quieted down after that," Barani grinned.

"How long have you had that gun?" I pointed at the pistol.

"I bought that damned thing the day after you moved out. I didn't want to believe what you told me, that somebody might try to come after you." Gracie looked over her shoulder at the blood on the floor and shuddered. "I don't ever want to see it again."

"There's three bullets missing," Barani said. "One was recovered from the wall. I'm sure the other two are in our suspect."

"Damn, girl," I said. "Remind me never to piss you off."

"You already know better than to piss me off, Niccolo." She smiled at me as she wrapped her arms around me and laced her fingers together at my side. "Just get me out of here tonight."

*****

By early Thursday afternoon, I was sitting beside Alicia Linnerman at the police station, watching via computer, as Poole, his calf wrapped in bandages and one arm resting on his crutches, sat stone-faced in front of Barnes. Numbers in the screen's lower corner ticked off rapidly as the conversation, or lack of it, was recorded.

"How's your wife, Fitz?" Alicia stared at the computer.

"She's really shook up, but she's going to be OK."

Alicia pointed to the computer screen. "Why do you think Poole targeted you?"

"We'd figured out the photo on his cellphone — the one that was supposedly taken at his daughter's birthday party the day Gina was killed—was falsely or incorrectly dated. I don't know whether Ambrosi turned that information over to you or if he was obligated to, so don't bitch at me. If he has to, I'm sure he will," I said. "I'm assuming Poole had no idea about Rachel's confession—he just knew his alibi for killing Gina was now officially shot in the ass and he wanted to do whatever it took to get me off the case."

"That makes sense."

"What about Dennis Lance?"

Alicia sighed. "He's off the hook with Gina's murder, of course—he had no idea Gina was coming to the house. Professionally, he's pretty damaged. He's calling off the run for judge and he's taking a leave of absence from the prosecutor's office. I've been appointed interim prosecutor until he decides what he's going to do next."

"Congratulations. Do you think you'll run for his job?"

Alicia grimaced. "I don't want to think about running for his office right now. I really liked Dennis. I respected him. His term wasn't up for another year, so I've got a while to make my decision—it's too painful to think about right now. I'm just amazed at how Rachel was able to pull the whole thing off."

"And speaking of Rachel, what's going on with her?"

"She had a hearing this morning. The judge ordered her held without bond, so she'll be sitting in jail for a while. We're confident the charges we brought against her will stand. We're also contacting Summit County about possible manslaughter charges in her father's suicide—against her and her mother."

So the enigma that was Rachel would finally be exposed. She had been an unanswerable question, a delicious unattainable goddess to anyone who saw her, even her husband who got drawn in to her mystery. But her secrets would have destroyed both her marriage and their future. Those secrets were all reopened with the discovery of her sister Gina. As much as Rachel may have claimed she wanted to help, it was pretty clear her motives were not entirely altruistic. Gina needed to be out of town and out of Dennis Lance's line of sight to assure his wife could keep her secrets and his career could advance.

I still had a couple questions, though.

"So tell me, what was the connection between Jorge Rivera and Reno Elliot?"

"We think the connection began with Jacob and Reno, probably through the heroin trafficking—we've got investigators on that right now. We think Reno intimidated Gina to keep her quiet, but couldn't report directly back to Jacob without tipping off the chief, so went through Jorge. And just for the record, Rivera was a federal CI, not a local one."

"Did you figure out where Poole killed Gina?"

"We have an idea. Poole and Rivera left the Lance house with Gina in Rivera's pick-up truck. We didn't have Rivera in our radar for obvious reasons, but after Rachel spilled her guts, police began a search for his truck last night and found it abandoned in a ditch outside of town. There's blood in the truck bed we believe is Gina's, along with a tarp Poole wrapped her in. Somehow they managed to get the body back behind the stage in the dark. There were a lot of service vehicles parked behind the stage Sunday and it was dark. It's possible no one saw the two of them bring her in. She was very tiny. Wrapped in a tarp no one would have known what was going on."

"But why put her back at the festival?"

Alicia shrugged. "We're not sure. The only thing we can think is that Poole knew she'd argued with Mike Atwater and he was trying to pin her death on him."

I shook my head. Poor, poor Gina: in her efforts to stand up for her wrongly accused father, she'd been completely destroyed by the people who should have helped her, her sister and her mother. She wasn't a world-class manipulator like them, and the men in her life played her more than she played them, even ignorant Mike Atwater. Maybe if she'd taken Rachel up on her offer for rehab, she would have had at least one chance in life. What held her back? The possibility of losing her children? Maybe she thought, too, she was protecting them by putting locks on the outside of their bedroom doors, so they wouldn't see Jacob Poole and his cohorts cutting up the heroin in her living room.

I was silent for a moment before asking my next question.

"Then who shot Rivera?"

Alicia pointed at Jacob on the computer monitor. "This guy. He hasn't given Barnes anything—he's going to lawyer up any second now. But we can string enough of a case together to charge him with Jorge's murder, along with Gina's. He'll also face intimidation charges, along with trafficking, not to mention breaking and entering charges for what happened at your place."

"Any ideas on who set my place on fire?"

"Not yet."

We watched the computer monitor in silence for a few moments. The conversation between officer and suspect soon stalled, as Alicia predicted.

"I want to talk to my lawyer," Poole said in an electronically distorted voice. Barnes stood up and left the interrogation room. Momentarily, he was leaning against the doorframe where Alicia and I sat, case file in hand.

"You saw him lawyer up, counselor?"

"Yes, sir, I did." Alicia turned away from the monitor. "Go ahead and charge him, and read him his rights. We've got other things to do."

Barnes turned to me. "Before we go, I have to tell you, Fitz, you did a good job," he said. "See you in court this afternoon, counselor?"

I looked at Alicia, who nodded.

"We're dropping charges against Michael Atwater and seeking an indictment against Jacob Poole."

*****

"Who the fuck turned this into a goddamned Chamber of Commerce event?"

"Niccolo, shut the hell up!" My sister Chrissy smacked the back of my head as she passed by me, one arm clutching a basket with a huge casserole dish of ravioli inside. "It's Sunday and the priest from St. Rita's is in the corner, talking to Ma! Jesus Christ!"

It was three weeks later and I was, indeed, back in business. I'd found a former downtown bank building down the street from Ambrosi's office that was small enough for me to afford and in good enough shape to only require a couple coats of paint to make it respectable. "Fitzhugh Investigations" arched in gold lettering across the front window and fortunately for me, where the original vault still stood—and was locked—in the back. At night, I could store my customer files, my laptop and anything else of value where no errant bottle of flaming liquid could destroy all my work.

Chrissy walked toward the back of my new building, where two rows of folding tables covered with rented linens stood next to as many chairs as could be begged, borrowed or stolen from friends, family or places of worship. A third row of tables was groaning with food ranging from Ma's spaghetti and marinara, to salads, cakes, cannolis, and slow cookers filled with whatever ilk fed the masses at church socials and PTA suppers, cooked by my brothers' wives. Two punchbowls sat at the end of one of the tables.

The youngest of my nieces and nephews ran rampant through the office, behaving as only the Fitzhugh clan does: at decibels that strained the eardrums and at speeds up to one hundred miles an hour. The older ones were still away at college and couldn't be here, the lucky little bastards; the preteens were sulking someplace, I assumed, passing time with their video games and simmering hormones.

The other adult male Fitzhughs—both those born into the clan and those who married into it—hung around two huge coolers of beer, talking baseball as my sisters and sisters-in-law fiddled around the food tables.

"Jesus, kids—Uncle Nicco needs some silence!" I called out. "Is it too early to teach you guys how to drink and smoke so you'll have something quiet to do in a corner?"

Gracie stopped adjusting my tie and pressed a finger against my mouth. "Sssshhh, Niccolo," she whispered. "Your mother bought your membership in the Chamber this year. They thought a ribbon cutting would be a great way to say you were back in business."

There were distinct divisions in the open space: my glassed-in office, a wide lobby I would use as a waiting room and, along the back in front of the vault, what had been the teller counter, today covered with cards from well-wishers. On a weekend foray into Amish country, Gracie found an executive desk, a nice leather chair for my office and overstuffed couch and chairs for the waiting room.

Well-wishers, many of them cops I worked with and courthouse staff, walked in and out, filling their plates with food.

"We need to go say thank you to everyone who came by to see you," Gracie said, dusting off the shoulders of my suit jacket. "And mind your mouth."

In the next thirty minutes I did as my lovely bride said, shaking every one's hand and thanking them for coming. For the first time in a long time, life was good. Gracie and I continued to be happy and once again, we'd taken our place in the Fitzhugh Sunday pasta dinner rotation.

Thanks to Mike Atwater's case, the work was pouring in: On Monday, when I officially opened, I had a full calendar for the entire week. Not just cases where I was rousting spouses from beds they weren't supposed to be in, but a fairly decent number of attorneys wanting me to investigate insurance claims or do defense work.

Yes, life was good.

"Niccolo!" Ma, leaning on the priest's arm, waved me toward the front door. "It's time to take your picture!" Dutifully, the family filed outside for the ribbon-cutting photo. When it appeared in the *Times* the following week, the photographer caught me planting a kiss on the side of Gracie's head as pieces of cut ribbon fluttered to the ground.

After the picture, I noticed Alicia Linnerman standing off to the side, sipping punch from a paper cup.

"Hello there," I said, hugging her. "Thanks for stopping by."

"Wouldn't have missed it for the world," she answered. "I have a little news for you too. We're charging Jacob Poole with ordering the firebombing on your place. We arrested two members of Road Anarchy last night, one of them Charlie Horton; he said they did it on Poole's orders."

"Awesome."

"And Fitz?"

"Yeah?"

"I'm giving up on bad boys—and I'm running for prosecutor."

"I don't know which one of those three makes me happiest." I smiled. She hugged me and, tossing the paper cup in the trash, left my office. I watched her walk down the sidewalk toward the courthouse.

Gracie stepped next to me and slid her hand into mine.

"Who's that?"

"Somebody who's knows when life is good, just like me."

About the author

Debra Gaskill is an award-winning journalist with more than 20 years experience in newspapers in Ohio. She has an associate's degree in liberal arts from Thomas Nelson Community College in Hampton, Va., a bachelor's degree in English and journalism from Wittenberg University and a master of fine arts degree in creative writing from Antioch University.

She and her husband Greg, a retired Air Force lieutenant colonel, reside in Enon, where they raise llamas and alpacas on their farm. They have two adult children and two grandchildren

She is the author of five Jubilant Falls novels, *The Major's Wife, Barn Burner, Lethal Little Lies, Murder on the Lunatic Fringe* and *Death of a High Maintenance Blonde.* This is the first novel in her *Fitz* series.

Connect with Debra on her website at www.debragaskillnovels.com or on her blog, http://debragaskill.wordpress.com. You can also connect with her on Twitter at @Debra Gaskill.

If you liked *Call Fitz,* please leave a review on the website where you purchased it. Your support is greatly appreciated!

Acknowledgements

As always, I am deeply indebted to those folks who guide my journey: my editors, who are authors in their own rights, Mary McFarland and Doug Savage. They guided me through this process with enthusiasm and support, and who weren't afraid to tell me when I wrote crap. I also want to thank Paul Schaffer, my copy editor extraordinaire. All three of them know better than anyone how to slap a noun up against a verb and make them both squeal.

I would also like to thank the members of the Southern Ohio Writers and Readers Collaborative, who told me what kind of guns to use, when my story went off track and when to keep going. You are all a blessing to me.

Thanks to a certain unnamed private detective, who offered insight on the true life of a private investigator, and to Jennica Stout, who took an entire afternoon to show me the best way to commit arson.

Made in the USA
Columbia, SC
12 June 2022